's Perch
Gellian Forest
Triad Hills
le of Empyrean
Viridian
AEGEAS FIELD
Mt. Venias
Fortuitus
Shrine of Astria
Eleapas
Nassau
Boreaux
Temple of Vedrah
lines
Barrae
Thomas Bay
Amethyst
Misty Jungle
NRIKK'S GORGE
Eastern Mines
Calig
Revale
Thom's Bridge
Cleopa
n Mines
Vedrah's Tail
Wellister
Urias
DOVER
Corva Isles
Katarina
Aiken
The Empire of Arkania

The Avat Prince

VOLUME FIVE

Copyright © 2024 House MVP

Cover art and interior illustrations © Myranda V. Peterson
House MVP Logo © Myranda V. Peterson
The Avat Prince: Tales of Arkania Skits © Myranda V. Peterson

Cartography brushes used in map artwork designed by Joel Pigou
https://www.gumroad.com/joelpigou

ISBN 9781957330099

First Edition Printed March 2020
MVP TV Edition Printed July 2024

Printed by IngramSpark in the USA.

House MVP
16 Thomas Patten Dr., P.O. Box 21
Randolph, MA, 02368

https://www.housemvpmedia.com

The text of this book is set in 12-point Adobe Garamond Pro.

*For all who've bounced back. You're not who you were.
You're becoming who you were meant to be.*

the Avat Prince

VOLUME FIVE

WRITTEN AND ILLUSTRATED BY

MYRANDA V. PETERSON

THE AVAT PRINCE:
TALES OF ARKANIA

To access locked skits for
THE AVAT PRINCE:

First, get reading!

When you see the word 'TV' at the end of a
sentence, it's time for a skit!

Illustrations are paired off with these pages.
Scan an illustration's QR code to access its skit.

Enter the password.

Enjoy the show!

(Don't forget to come back to keep reading the story!)

MVP
TV

HOUSE MVP

Previously in The Avat Prince...

Now an auction raid trainee, Brent at last feels empowered. By studying under the ex-gladiator Jeffrey, he has taken a step forward in embracing his new freedom and sharing it with others.

Meanwhile, in the faraway heart of the Empire, a young Emperor Koberius Arkania wrestles with the imperial god Empyrean that possesses his body. But, no matter how strong his will is, he can never bring himself to withstand the deity's strangling desire for carnage. So he succumbs to the spirit's urging, and loses a part of himself every time. But to what end does the imperial god lust for blood?

Six years go by and Brent finally graduates as a slave auction raider. He vows to free the Avat slaves and grant them sanctuary like Adelle did for him, but when he visits her grave he has a vision of an aetherial world filled with green and gold mist, and glimpses a man with trailing, sky-blue hair. As quickly as the vision appears it's gone, leaving Brent with a myriad of questions.

Meanwhile, the Shrine of Astria has answered Emperor Koberius' call and recruits a young woman, a Daughter of Astria, to house the spirit of the imperial god Vedrah. Together they seek bloodshed, all to bring about the undoing of "Zion's curse".

Elsewhere, far across the sea, the masked stranger who spoke with Xëri, Oruviçu, returns to his island and reports to Elder Qaçai, a red-haired Avat who oddly has the turquoise eyes of an aetheriest. Oruviçu himself, while also an Avat, bears the cosmic gaze of an aetherian. But how is this possible when stories say that Avats can't harness the power of the aether?

Oruviçu shares details about Brent with the elder, and adds that he may have gained the attention of Çaru'qu, a spirit that has slumbered for millennia and is stirred by the blood that Empyrean and Vedrah shed. But why has this spirit taken an interest in Brent?

Brent isn't even aware of it. But one thing is clear: the Empire nurses more evil and more secrets than its racial injustices.

THE VALLEY OF TARANIS
YEAR 467 OF THE ARKANIAN IMPERIAL CALENDAR
SO...
THIS...IS WHERE THEY BURIED YOU.
FSWW...
....

ADELLE...
HEY, ORVIS...
Y'KNOW, ORVIS...
IT'S GOOD TO SEE YOU, ORVIS!
I...

PLIP
PLOP
I SHOULD'VE BEEN THERE.

MOVE IT!
UGH!
^PUFF^
^HUFF^
^HUFF^
^PUFF^

YOU! WHO SAID YOU COULD TAKE A BREAK?!
P-PLEASE, I --
CRACK!!
AGH!
WE'VE GOT A QUOTA TO FILL!!
YOU MISS THE QUOTA, YOU MISS YOUR MEAL!!

DASH!
TATATA
?
WHOOSH!
WHUD!!
?!
....

WHIRL
CATCH!
TATATATA
TATATATA

34

THE RING OF pickaxes echoed between the tiered walls of the quarry. The crack of whips crashed over them, along with the shouts of overseers who were annoyed by the Avat slaves and their dragging feet. Hurling insults, they shoved the enslaved to get them to march faster with their sacks of earth, or to cart even heavier loads to the upper levels of the mine and boost workday productivity.

Only some responded by doubling their pace. But most could barely keep the speed at which they were moving, what with their fatigue and the blistering heat. It was summer all across the southern regions of the Arkanian Empire and the weather was worse here, in the Southern Mines of Lenora Province. Most of the central province was practically a desert wasteland but in the south, with the Trevian Desert only a few leagues to the north, the air was scorching. When paired with the giant pillars of crystal, emerald, and other precious rocks that burst out of the ground and reflected the heat, it became that much more unbearable.

There were only a few shaded areas that offered relief. Arranged on certain levels of the quarry, they were stations that had been designated for slaves to break ore deposits and free all sorts of stones: anthracite and onyx, or strains of silver and gold to be pounded into the imperial coinage, the arkan. Every now and then another slave would come along, gather these stones into a sack, and carry them over to others who were preparing to wheel loads of it to the higher levels for distribution. After casting their burdens onto this party, they'd turn back and start the process again.

Above them soldiers ringed the mining perimeter, casting their visored eyes to and fro to watch for potential outbreaks of rebellion. Their spears were in hand, at the ready, and though the sun tried to grill them through their armor they retained their stoicism.

Otherwise they cared little for the slaves, who struggled through their dreadful, repetitious work. But at the very least it fed them, even if they were only given scraps or were forced to huddle around a trough and spoon slop into their mouths once a day. Many of them considered themselves lucky to have at least that — it was better than starving to death in the back roads of the provincial capital nearby.

And yet it was nearly high noon, and none of them had eaten for hours. Some fantasized about water as they worked. Others longed to collapse from exhaustion but didn't, for fear of being whipped or beaten.

"Faster, you blasted devils!" an overseer bellowed, cracking his whip near a line of Avats who were carrying sacks of rocks across their shoulders. Their dark skin glistened in the daylight and their hair lay plastered against their brows. Some, bearing scars from previous beatings, struggled to obey. *"Faster!"*

Almost out of his line of sight, a young girl dropped the sack that she'd been carrying. Desperate yet knowing that it was too heavy for her, she tried to drag it across the ground.

But it ripped, and piles of glittering rocks spilled out.

She yelped, then screamed when the overseer grabbed her by the hair.

"You goblins just can't figure it out!" he growled and he threw her to the ground.

She landed in a heap.

No sooner had she fallen did the overseer crack his whip at her.

But another slave shielded her, and it coiled around his forearm instead.

"We beg pardon." The young man spoke in a quiet voice, meaning to evoke a sense of calm that would deescalate the situation. A low hood covered his head, shading his pale skin from the terrible sun, and strands of golden hair hovered just above his downturned eyes. He wore a tattered cowl and his forearms were reinforced with leather greaves that looked worn with wear. Fortunately, the whip had cracked around one of these arm bands, sparing his skin. "She was just trying to work faster, like you asked."

"Don't talk back to me!" Winding his whip, the overseer cracked it again.

This time the young man ducked, dropping to one knee with his hands clasped as if in urgent prayer. "Please," he begged gently. He quickly cast an arm out in front of the girl. "Please."

The overseer growled at him. Beneath his galea helmet his gray eyes flitted between the two, as if he was debating whether or not to inflict some kind of punishment for them to share.

Without warning, he kicked the young man over.

With a grunt the slave collapsed in front of the girl, who jumped with a startled squeak. His bucket, full of precious stones, fell to the ground and several spilled out.

"Keep it in check, slave," the soldier sneered and he marched away to supervise the rest of the quarry. "And I better not hear you talking again!"

The little girl hesitated and fearfully glanced between the departing soldier and her rescuer. Turning to the latter, she managed to ask, "A-a-are you okay?"

The young man sighed and shook his head to free the sand and dirt from his eyes. "I'm fine." He looked at her. "But what about you? You're not hurt?"

Now that he was looking up at her, the girl could see his face in its entirety. Her eyes grew.

His pale, silver irises nearly vanished into the whites of his eyes. It was ghostlike, but captivating.

For a short second, she wondered if he was blind. In the next, she wondered if he was even an Avat?

She couldn't tell. His hood hid his ears.

But she didn't think he was, given his eyes. So far as she knew, Avats had dark, almond-shaped eyes and brown skin — the shade ranged — as well as protruding cheekbones. Their jet-black hair was straight, long and coarse, though most of the time it was frizzy from work. As for their ears, which was their most telling feature, they extended into sharp points and offered their owners the ability to hear things that no round-eared Arkanian could.

Aside from his angular face, this man didn't have any Avat features. Maybe he was just a regular Arkanian who'd been caught fraternizing with goblins — "sympathizers", as the imperials called them — and had been sold into slavery as punishment.

She felt bad for him.

And guilty.

Suddenly the young man got up, derailing her train of thought. He extended his hand to her. "Here."

"Th…thank you." Taking it, she got to her feet and looked into his face timidly.

He smiled faintly. She almost missed it. "Go. I'll take care of this," he added when she looked at her broken sack.

Casting him one last, curious look, she hurried away.

Without another word, the young man watched her go. He didn't turn when he heard someone else come up behind him.

"I hate overseers," the person grunted.

The young man shifted to see him.

It was another Avat, one who was pushing a wheelbarrow full of sand, dirt and dull stones. With a plain wrap tied around his head and a cloth thrown over his bare shoulders, he scowled after the imperial that had nearly lashed the little girl.

He was clearly a mixed blood, with olive skin, a short button nose and dazzling blue eyes. A small mole was printed just beneath the right one, and locks of wavy red hair curled out from beneath his wrap. Slightly shorter than his blonde friend, his body was well-trained and lean, and like many of the other slaves he was glowing with sweat.

"And I hate groveling at their feet," the hooded slave replied darkly. He, too, turned to look at the distancing overseer. "But at least that girl isn't hurt."

"Yeah. Nice save." The redhead glanced at him and nodded at his clothes. "How's the heat?"

"Being an Avat with albinism has its downsides," his hooded ally replied, "but Khirsta's special sunblock hasn't failed me yet.

Still" — he cast his friend a sarcastic smile — "it's nice to see you care."

"Yeah, right," the redhead scoffed. "The last thing we need is you breaking out in the middle of a mission. I don't envy you one bit."

"Most don't. But albinism has its upsides, too." The hooded Avat went silent for a moment, his ears picking through the clamor of mining tools and shouting until he discerned what he was looking for.

It came from the tunnels that burrowed deep into the quarry walls above them: feet racing through the dark in animal-hide shoes; the twirl of a staff; the grunt of an imperial when he was knocked out before he'd even realized what was happening —

And a quiet rumbling through the mine walls, like an incoming earthquake.

He tuned it all out. "He's almost here. Sounds like the tunnels are about to go, too."

"Good. This thing itches." As if to prove his point, the redhead stuck his hand beneath his wrap and scratched his scalp. "Can't wait to take it off."

"And the upper ring?" his hooded friend continued, not looking at him.

"Everyone's in position," the redhead answered. "Just gotta wait for his cue."

"Hey! You two there!"

The redhead turned; his hooded friend simply moved his eyes.

Another overseer was marching towards them. "Quit lagging! Get to work or I'll —"

A tunnel in the wall above them exploded, vomiting smoke and fire like a volcanic belch.

A topless, brown-skinned figure flew out of it, practically riding the explosion's force. With a long staff in one hand, he landed atop a wooden pillar and perched there.

The smoke cleared around him, revealing his beaded necklaces, patterned pants and tasseled waist sashes. As he lifted his head it shied away from his blue hair next, and carefully unveiled his pointy ears. When the sunlight struck them, his golden eyes danced.

Spotting the overseer, he grinned wolfishly.

What happened next took a second:

The hooded Avat reached beneath the front of the wheelbarrow and drew the sword that had been strapped to its underbelly. "Aaron —"

"He's always gotta be so dramatic…!" The red-haired Avat, Aaron, thrust his hands into the rocks he'd been pushing around and yanked out a twin pair of tonfa —

The overseer's eyes bulged as he gaped at the staff-wielding Avat. "S-Skylok!" he blurted, recalling the criminal's infamous name scrawled upon wanted posters everywhere. He whirled to a watchtower that was caught in the shadow of one of the quarry's tiers. "S-sound the alarm! Savages are —!"

He broke off when the front head of a tonfa smashed into the side of his helmet, knocking him out.

With a flourish of his weapon, Aaron looked up from his felled opponent.

A group of soldiers were sprinting down one of the quarry ramps towards him, spears out.

Clicking his tongue, he pressed the buttons in his handlebars, right by his thumbs.

Instantly, the shafts of his tonfa retracted and the short swords that were hidden inside of them shot out.

He flipped them along the length of his arms, and they flashed angrily. "Liam!"

"Ahead of you." Silvery eyes bright, Liam flourished his sword.

Together, they charged at the incoming soldiers.

Overhead, the golden-eyed Avat hopped from one wooden pillar to another and then jumped into the watchtower. Just before the soldier inside could swing his mallet and strike the alarm bell, he twirled out from behind it and batted him unconscious.

As the imperial's body dropped, he looked up.

A new pair of soldiers were running at him, their sandaled feet pounding against the wooden bridge that connected the watchtower to a structure of scaffolding.

He sighed. "They never just let us walk out."

Still, with a daring smile, he spun his staff behind his back and grabbed its upper half as if it were the grip of a sword. Rushing to meet the imperials he twisted the upper half of his staff and pulled, unsheathing it from its bottom piece and revealing the swords that had been locked inside.

Drawing them out fully he jumped and spun between the soldiers, striking them with a winding blow and sending them toppling off the bridge.

Blades out he landed on one knee, then leaped to the ground after them.

"Brent," Aaron greeted dryly, batting an overseer to the ground. He stood back-to-back with him. "You just had to make an entrance, didn't you?"

"Keeps 'em guessin'!" the warrior returned, smiling.

Brent — known to the imperials by his outlaw title, "Skylok", thanks to his reputation as a slave auction raider and liberator of Avat slaves — parried an imperial, dashed his spear to pieces, and struck him down with a heavy blow.

"They finally gave me an outlaw name," he said. "I can't just waltz in!"

"Yeah, yeah, whatever." Aaron ducked beneath a sword and on coming back up he slammed the sharp heads of his tonfa through the overseer's tunic, ripped them out — drawing ribbons of crimson with them — and kicked him over. "Attention-hog."

"You're just grumpy cuz you *don't* have a cool nickname." Brent countered a soldier and, taking the man's spear with his swords, he spun it and bashed him over the head with it once, twice, then he locked his weapon back into its full-length form and struck him down.

The man hit the ground like a spinning missile.

Brent refaced Aaron, hardly missing a beat. "Ain't that right? Speedy Two-Sticks."

"It's *Blaze!*" Aaron fired back. Wall-kicking off of a scaffolding, he flipped over an imperial. Grabbing the man's head in mid-flight, he rotated, landed, and slammed him into the ground.

"Blowin' off steam there, buddy?"

"Shut up."

"Guys." Liam twisted an overseer's arm, broke it, and tossed his screaming form aside. "Focus."

"Yeah, focus, Aaron," Brent chided.

"He's talking to *you!*" Aaron snapped as he moved on to another section of the quarry.

Snickering, Brent brought his fingers to his lips and whistled.

Knowing that to be their cue, teams of men and women — Arkanians and Avats alike — came pouring out of some of the tunnels on the upper rings. Armed with wide-bladed swords, curved daggers and spears, they were dressed similarly to Brent: hand-painted patterns adorned their waist sashes and baggy pants; armlets glittered on their biceps; beads and cuffs twinkled in their hair. They were undoubtedly foreign to the lands of Arkania.

Catching the quarry's overseers off guard, they fell upon them like a pack of dicani. Weapons flashed and bodies dropped — it was like a full-out war had erupted in the quarry.

Elsewhere, at the mouth of a ground-level tunnel where a group of men had been hauling out a hunk of marble, an Avat woman drew a dagger from the sheath that was hidden beneath her dress and slew an overseer that was just behind her.

Tearing her hair out of its bun, she lifted her gleaming weapon high. Her skin shone with just as much fervor as it did.

"Now!" she yelled, her dark eyes ablaze, and the slaves behind her turned from their task, hammers and pickaxes bared, and they charged at the slave drivers with cries of war.

Startled, the foremen either backpedaled or froze. One tried cracking his whip at at the oncoming crowd.

His attempt was successful: a man fell over with a bleeding gash across his face.

But the overseer hadn't been able to stop the uprising. Indeed, he was jumped on by a pair of rebels, one Avat and one Arkanian. Their combined weight sent him crashing to the ground.

At the same time, a tunnel that overlooked the quarry suddenly exploded. Rubble roared within as it collapsed.

Not even a second later, another passage suddenly collapsed on itself, as if of its own accord.

"Get to the exit!" one of the foreign warriors yelled, pointing his sword at one of the tunnels. At ground level, it was fixed between a mountain of worthless rocks and rickety scaffolding.

"Head them off!" a soldier roared as the attackers began to ferry the slaves into the passage. "Cut them down if you have to, don't let them escape!"

Taking out another guard with a wide spin of his staff, Brent cast his eyes across the battlefield. Not far away, he spotted an ally in a tight scuffle with an overseer: the young Avat was armed with a bow while his enemy had a sword.

Seeking to help, Brent stomped on the edge of a javelin that was at his feet and caught it. Muscles flexing, he hurled it at the overseer.

The spear hit him right between the shoulder blades, and in his paralysis the archer grappled him with his legs and flipped him to the ground. In the same movement, he nocked an arrow into his bow, took aim and fired at the quarry bell.

It tolled noisily.

There was a breath of silence.

Then the ground shook.

"Fall back!" Brent thundered, and he pulled something out of the back folds of one of his sashes. It was a small, silver pole.

Flicking a switch that was on it he threw it at the soldiers who were still coming. Hissing furiously, it released a cloud of gray smoke that made the imperials stop short.

All along the defensive line that protected the escaping slaves, warriors threw down similar items that added to the sprawling smoke.

Hesitating, the soldiers who'd been trying to force their way through their defenses stopped, wary of the smog as if it were a coiling vapor of poison.

"After them!" one of the commanding officers finally shouted, kicking a subordinate into the gray. It closed around him like a set of wispy, winding arms.

A second later, the man flew out of the cloud like he'd been fired from a cannon. Screaming, he crashed through a scaffolding some distance away.

Wearing expressions that ranged from shock to fear, the soldiers peered into the smoke, watchful and waiting.

A moment later a soft wind blew it all away, revealing the tunneled opening in the wide wall.

The barbarians and the slaves were gone. Now, only a woman remained at the mouth of the passage: pale-skinned and round-eared, she was graced with a head of silky, green hair that billowed around her frame. Evidently she was Lenoran, but she was dressed as exotically as those who'd infiltrated the quarry.

Squaring her shoulders, she stood flat-footed before the remaining imperials. Hands already outstretched, she took a breath.

On her exhale the air pulsed, and a bodiless weight pressed against the soldiers from seemingly everywhere.

Someone cursed.

"An aetheriest!" another man shouted.

"Kill her! Get to those slaves!"

The woman spoke no words. Her green eyes burning with resolve, she waved her right arm across the air.

The earth shifted, rolled like ocean waves. Then a flurry of stalagmites erupted from the ground, blocking her from view and covering the mouth of the tunnel.

No sooner had she conjured the rocky barrier did another tunnel spontaneously collapse with a terrible bellow, followed by another, and then another. Then sections of the quarry itself began to detonate, blowing scaffoldings apart and blasting rocks everywhere. Tremors ran through the earth with every eruption, forcing the imperials to lose their footing, and as their whole world crumbled to dust around them, they screamed.

But over the roar of destruction, no one could hear them.

35

LAUGHING HEARTILY, CHIEF Anania crashed her mug of drink against Brent's and then downed it in a few short gulps. He did the same.

All around them the men and women who'd participated in the attack on the Southern Mines were just as cheerful, passing drinks or conversing in loud voices as they recounted some of their favorite parts of the fighting. Those they'd rescued from their grueling labor seemed alert at best, almost overwhelmed by the fact that they were now out of imperial clutches. Caught between relief and anxiety, they didn't even seem to trust that everything they were witnessing was real, or if the heat of the day had finally gotten to them.

But as they ate real food and drank liquids that not only quenched their thirst but left their tastebuds buzzing, they could only bring themselves to believe one thing: this was real.

They were *free.*

With a low laugh, Anania sighed. She'd been a part of the raid — in fact had been the face that had ended it with her aetherial abilities and had sealed their exit while the quarry had collapsed.

"I owe you, *Skylok,*" she said, smiling at Brent. Her voice, low and husky, carried a slight twang to it that was reminiscent of all those who lived across the southern regions of Lenora Province. But it was subtle. Were he not at least part-Avat, Brent was sure he wouldn't have even noticed it. "This raid wouldn't have been a success without you, or your unit. I'm glad Chief Ivan let us borrow you for the last few days."

"It's not like it was all us," Brent said, a twinkle in his eye, and he looked out to the celebration. "You've got some pretty good raiders here already."

Anania laughed, pulling his eyes back to her. "But none as wild as you. When Chief Ivan sent word that he had someone who could help us stop those miners from digging any closer to our tunnels, I didn't wanna believe him. Then you showed up, and had the audacity to suggest that we connect one of our tunnels to the mines, collapse the rest, and lead the slaves back through to our home here. I'll admit we hadn't even considered that as a strategy. The tunnels leading to this place're tricky, to say the least. If you hadn't brought the aetheriests that you had to help me, I doubt we would've been able to pull it off.

"You're a bright one." She tipped her cup to him. "You're just what the Liberation Fronts need at a time like this, what with Empyrean's Guard around: daring, but strategic. It's no wonder I've been hearing all that good news about Taranis lately, what with you leadin' one successful raid after another. I'm just glad you were willin' to share your luck with us."

"Eh, it's no big deal. The Liberation Fronts' mission is the same at every location. We help our own." He twice pounded a fist against his left breast, over his heart, saluting her the same way Chief Ivan would have given his Katruskik heritage. "Besides, I've never been to Dukaris," he added, looking around the massive, underground cavern that they were in presently. "This place is amazing!"

Indeed, the location for the Liberation Front of Dukaris was a daunting space. Given that it was underground it provided respite from the terrible heat above, and it boasted vaulted ceilings, yawning passageways and towering columns of rock that connected ground to roof. Hardly any stalactites ruptured the ceiling there, but all across its surface existed a countless number of glowing stones hidden in the rock. Offering a calm, blue light, they illuminated the stony village below.

Houses had been carved out of the walls, with some standing

on ledges while others protruded over the domed level that acted as a community hall. Stairs curved towards some, ladders towards others, and from the higher homes ropes dangled to offer a faster descent.

Farther away, tunnels that were large enough to have allowed the entry of giants burrowed deeper into the caves, their curving walls sparkling with the same gentle light that fell from on high. A river coursed through one of them, spilling from a waterfall that gushed out of the rock on the other side of the chamber.

As for the community hall, it was the liveliest spot. A low cavern with multiple archways and natural columns, it was illuminated by the very same gems that filled the rest of the sanctuary, and the rocky floor was smooth to the point of polish. The waterfall that fed the subterranean river gushed just beyond one of the exits, spraying the area with a cooling mist, and the jubilant sounds of laughter and banter resounded all the while.

Towards the front of the area a band of villagers were playing drums and bells in celebration of the raiders' successful return, creating a thrumming atmosphere of energy. One of them had even constructed a qora, a double-bridge-harp-lute that added a layer of rippling acoustics to the joyous melody. All around them, stone pillars with flames dancing inside of azure crystals added extra light, casting excited shadows all across the cave walls.

"They say these tunnels used to be an underground bunker, before the Empire was ever even around," Anania recalled. "Back when the continent was so war-torn you couldn't take half a step without gettin' blasted by an aetherian."

"Huh." Brent flashed his eyebrows as he took the place in. "And whoda thought they'd be right under Cleopa?"

"Yup." Anania smiled again, mischievously this time. "Empyrean's Guard still ain't thought to go lookin' underground for us 'savage villages'. I expect things to stay that way."

"Brent."

Both Brent and Anania turned.

Liam was coming towards them.

Though they were now in the cooler caverns of Dukaris he hadn't changed out of his imperial wear, instead keeping to his hooded cowl, as well as a pair of scrunched trousers and sandals. His hood was off though, freeing his pointy ears and revealing his head of blonde-yellow hair, whose split bangs fell towards his eyes. His wide-bladed sword was holstered to the back of his waist, and his complimentary dagger was belted to his left thigh.

"Trent should be coming along the royal highway soon." A hot bowl of mushrooms and cave fish in hand — a popular dish in Dukaris — he came to a stop in front of the pair, who were standing atop a natural dais that hunched out of the earth. "We can't stick around for much longer."

"Right." Brent nodded. "Cool as it is to finally see Lenora, we wouldn't wanna miss our ride out. You seem pretty eager to go yourself."

"I'm grateful for the hospitality of Dukaris. And you, Chief." Liam acknowledged Anania. "But if we're not out of Cleopa by nightfall, we'll be stuck in Lenora 'til we can contact another supporter. At that point we'd be risking capture. Sooner we're out of the city, the better."

"Straight-shooter, just like Chief Ivan said." Anania smiled crookedly. "Guess there's no way I can talk ya'll into stickin' around for a little while longer?"

"Sorry. No."

Anania's smile became regretful, but understanding.

"Leave it to Liam to keep us on track." Brent shrugged. "But if he didn't do it, no one would."

"Cuz you guys'd be too busy with stupid arguments," Liam said. He actually smiled a little. "Like whose outlaw name is better."

"I had to live up to my title! Not even a few months ago I was just 'some savage blue goblin'. I sounded like a dumb gnome."

Liam actually snorted.

"You're even laughing!"

"Wasn't," he denied.

"Yeah, right. Deadpan Liam just doesn't want anyone to know he's got a sense of humor."

"And now you're getting distracted."

"Gah, you're no fun…" Sighing, Brent faced Anania, who stood just a head shorter than him. "Well, take care of yourselves. And don't hesitate to reach out if you need help from your friends out west."

Anania gave a quick bob of her head before facing the party. "All of you, listen up!" she boomed, hoisting her mug.

Slowly, the room quieted to hear their chief.

"Tonight we celebrate a great victory, and the homecoming of our newest villagers," she started, her voice carried by the acoustics of the hall. "Tonight, we celebrate our continued success in liberating slaves across our region. And tonight, we remember our allies who've fallen in our noble fight. May we always remember their sacrifice, and the unity that it brings us!

"And may we always remember our family in Taranis, who lent us aid in our time of need." She turned to Brent. "Don't think that we'll forget this, my friend. If you ever have need of the warriors beneath the crags of Lenora, don't hesitate to reach out. On behalf of us all, and those who are now able to start their lives anew here: thank you."

She held out her hand and they clasped forearms.

Cheers and applause erupted from the crowd and with a smile Anania reached out to take Liam's arm as well, which he responded to in kind. No sooner had they shared their farewells did the music and jubilee start up again.*tv*

Brent and Liam descended from the dais and circled around the villagers, meaning to vacate the underground civilization. On the way, Brent caught the eyes of those who'd traveled with him from Taranis. With a slight nod, he ordered for them to follow.

Swallowing their last morsels of food and untangling themselves from whatever conversations that they were engaged in, they obeyed.

"Man, that rum they have here from Aiken is some good stuff!" Kro drawled in a cracking voice. His dimpled cheeks flushed with color, he stumbled alongside the group until he managed to gain some semblance of balance. The oldest of two Arkanian brothers, he was one of the most skilled aetheriests from Taranis, with messy brown hair, a broad-shouldered form and an aetherial versatility that made him more suitable for the inter-provincial mission than his younger sibling back home. "Who knew they had supporters

ANOTHER JOB WELL DONE
CODE: DUKARIS

all the way in Aiken? Why don't we have supporters all the way in Aiken?"

"Any supporters of Dukaris are supporters of Taranis," Brent reminded him as the small party of raiders and aetheriests marched towards a low tunnel at the back of the village. It was the only passage that was about as low as an average corridor, and two stone torches stood sentinel on either side of its entrance. "Besides, we've got people in Peluma, which is closer. Sometimes we get rum from them."

"But it's not the *saaame,*" Kro whined, dropping his shoulders and dragging his feet.

"You're a pain." Aaron scowled in his direction.

"You're just upset cuz I know how to have *fun!*"

Aaron gagged and recoiled, for Kro had huffed that last word right into his face. "Ugh, dude you reek! How much of that stuff did you drink?!"

"He had to have had at least four mugs' worth," said Kyrah, another aetheriest in the group. She was a petite Arkanian, with dark eyes and dark hair that she'd cut into a bob. Doubling as an intelligence scout for Taranis, Brent had recruited her to support Liam who, on top of auction raiding, had quickly proven his abilities as an intelligence agent not long after graduating into Taranis' forces. After all, being an Avat with albinism had its benefits: though he was far more sensitive to hot weather and sunlight compared to his darker counterparts and even suffered from irreparably poor vision, his hearing by far surpassed theirs. His appearance also allowed him to blend in with the general imperial populace — pair that with his ability to overhear conversations through buildings and across roads, and he was a prime spy.

Kyrah's skills, though not as impressive, were just as dependable, especially given that she was a few years older than Liam and thus had more experience under her belt.

"I thought for sure he was gonna barf it all up at one point," Rhea said, continuing their commentary. A young Arkanian woman, she was also an aetheriest, with long tresses of pitch-black hair raining to the small of her back. The beads that decorated her narrow hips clicked lightly as she walked.

"So did the guy sitting next to him," added the dark-skinned Avat archer trailing beside her. The youngest of the group he was Erikk, and had actually been the same warrior that Brent had assisted during the raid. "Especially when he started telling him about his days in the Aether Circus and got emotional."

"And then he started crying!" Kyrah remembered, laughing with him.

"I did not cry!" Kro protested. He stopped suddenly, his face blanking just as they entered the tunnel.

"Yeah, you did —" Kyrah started, only to jump back when Kro keeled over and vomitted.

Crying out, everyone near him retreated.

With a groan, Kro fell over, unconscious.

"I'm not carrying him." That said, Aaron stepped over Kro and marched into the darkness.

36

THE PASSAGE LEADING out of Dukaris was a winding one that opened into a massive, underground labyrinth. But, having received directions for it from the supporters who'd guided them to Dukaris initially, Brent and his party expected to make it through without trouble.

He and Liam took the helm, with Liam carrying a small stone that was like the rocks that lit Dukaris. A small fire was contained inside of it, and it threw dancing blue lights against the jagged walls as they walked along. Its heat was very much real; he could feel its warmth all over his hand.

The only one who suffered a slight lag in her speed was Kyrah, who'd volunteered to carry Kro through the aether as they went. The act was tiring, as she'd just expended much of her energy collapsing tunnels during the raid.

To her fortune Rhea soon spied her discomfort and offered her assistance. With his weight dispersed between their combined efforts, levitating him through the dark tunnels became that much easier.

"He should really cut back on the extra meat pies," Kyrah grimaced as she tromped forth, the sweat on her round face catching some of the light from Liam's glowing stone.

"That and your ability to influence is pretty low, given everything we just had to do," Rhea reminded her. "I'm running on fumes myself."

"Still." Kyrah's brow twisted; Kro bobbled a little in midair. "I know he wants to impress Renée with his muscle mass, but this is just ridiculous."

Ahead of them, Brent's ears twitched at the familiar name.

"Yeah…sometimes I feel sorta bad for him." Rhea cast Kro a sideways glance that was marked with pity. "He likes Ren a lot and he's really not a bad guy. But Ren's just not —"

She broke off when a figure suddenly appeared between them and hefted Kro over their shoulders.

It was Brent.

He flashed a smile at their startled looks, all while holding the aetheriest securely across his back. "Looked like you guys could use the help. We can't have three people collapse on us."

"Thanks," Kyrah gasped. "At this point, I was thinking about dragging him."

"Thank you," Rhea said.

Brent nodded and, adjusting his grip on Kro, he walked away.

Up ahead, Liam paused at a fork. There, with his silvery eyes lowered, he listened. His ears nearly rang in the quiet.

But soon he picked it out: the sound of voices.

He turned right.

"Think he overheard us?" Rhea asked Kyrah quietly once Brent was farther away.

She shrugged a shoulder.

"Think he's jealous?" Rhea asked, this time with a knowing smile.

Kyrah cocked an eyebrow. "You know how popular Brent is around Taranis. He doesn't have anything to be jealous of. Least of all of Kro."

"You're harsh," Rhea laughed then she straightened, her arms folding as she watched Brent up ahead of them. He was talking to Aaron now. "Maybe that's why Kro's trying so hard…" She sighed dreamily. "I wish a guy would try that hard with me…"

Kyrah laughed. "Honestly, Kro should give up while he's ahead. Maybe I should tell him you're available?"

"What? No, don't —!"

"But I thought you wanted a guy to win your affection!"

"I wanted it to happen naturally...!"

Kyrah laughed again.

Rhea huffed.

"And what're you ladies gossiping about?" Erikk suddenly asked, turning to look at them.

"Nothing," Rhea denied instantly. "Just girl talk."

"Right." Erikk tapped one of his pointy ears, reminding them of the innate listening skills of his race. "I gotcha. I won't say a thing. But Rhea, if you're looking for a bachelor I hear Duke talking about you a lot."

"Blech!" Rhea crinkled her nose at the thought of the older, plain-looking blacksmith from back home.

"And that right there is what'll keep you single," Kyrah teased.

Rhea groaned as Erikk joined in Kyrah's laughter.

At long last they came to the maze's final passage, which morphed into a set of stone stairs that carried them to the door of a cellar.

Liam pressed his ear against it for a split second. He heard nothing in the connecting room, so he opened the heavy barrier and went through first. The others followed.

Softer than a phantom he crossed the storage room that the door opened into, which was lined with cubbies of ale, mead and bedding, and made his way to a set of wooden stairs. Stuffing the blue rock beneath one of the cobbled stones that made up the floor, he flew up the steps and opened the trapdoor at the top to reveal a small, empty room.

The voices that he'd heard earlier were slightly louder now. Given that the building they'd entered was an inn and tavern, they likely belonged to evening patrons. Fortunately, they were far away enough that none of them would even glimpse him or his allies sneaking around.

So, he crawled into the open. One by one the others followed after him, and one by one they shadowed him to the nearest open-air doorway. Liam stopped in it for a second, listening, and when he heard no sign of onlookers from the connecting alley he signaled an all-clear.

Treading outside, the group found themselves in the backstreets of the farthest corners of the Lenoran capital.

Brent was the last to go, his speed hampered by his choosing to quietly close the trapdoor behind himself, rather than to let it slam. Once more adjusting his grip on Kro, he went after the others. But just before he could step outside he stopped and cast his golden eyes to the hallway on his left.

An Arkanian woman was making her way towards him from there, arms full of folded sheets and her disheveled, pink hair tied back by a colorful silk scarf. Surprise flitted across her middle-aged features when she spotted Brent in the doorway.

Freezing, she looked from him to the unconscious Kro draped over his shoulders.

"Oh — he drank too much," he explained, following her stare.

She gave him a baffled look, then chuckled. "You new generation of raiders sure are a handful, ain't ya?"

"No more than the older ones," Brent returned good-naturedly. His eyes twinkled in the soft light of evening. "Thanks, Legretta. For everything."

The woman bowed her head. "I'm glad everything turned out well. Give Chief Ivan my regards. The Waterhorse Inn is always open to your cause."

Brent smiled and, softer than the night, he disappeared through the doorway, leaving the woman to resume her course as if he'd never even been there.

Outside, Brent passed beneath the thatched awning that was attached to the inn's back wall. With Kro still in arm, he fixed his gaze on his allies who were waiting at a three-way fork just ahead.

As he neared them, Kro groaned and shifted on his shoulder. "Urgh…where am I…?"

Hearing him, Brent glanced back and dropped him like a travel sack.

"Ow!" Kro felt like his brains had scrambled. He swore.

"You overdid it," Brent said as Kro carefully got to his feet. While he spoke, he pulled what looked like an old piece of tattered fabric out of a hogshead and threw it on.

It was the cloak that he'd worn on their trip to Lenora, and had temporarily discarded just before entering Dukaris. Wrapping it about his throat and fastening it just beneath his left shoulder, it fell to his ankles and comfortably hid his village attire. As for his double-bladed staffs, he switched their placement so that one hung off of both of his hips. Thanks to his cloak, they were just as well-hidden.

"Better hope we don't run into any imperials on the way out," he finished, tossing his hood on. Hiding his ears, it cast his telling, golden eyes into shadow. Even with his head lifted, if one were to be at eye-level with him they'd only be able to see his nose and mouth. "In your condition, you'll probably hand yourself over."

"Would not!"

"But then we'd be about fifty thousand richer, right? For getting a 'savage' off the streets?" Kyrah looked to Rhea for confirmation, who nodded thoughtfully.

"Don't sell me out — *hic!*"

"Guess this is why the chief says that raiders shouldn't drink on missions," Erikk said, studying Kro as he got up.

"Especially not the young ones," Kyrah added. "Don't follow his example. Your brain'll be a puddle by the time you're his age."

"Please." The aetheriest's eyes were heavily shadowed, as if he hadn't had a full night's rest. He didn't seem completely sober yet, either. "I pride myself on my tolerance level."

"And your sense of balance, no doubt." Kyrah nodded at his unsteady feet.

"He did wake up kinda fast, though," Erikk admitted.

"Judging by the sun, we've only got so much time to get to the outer wall before the gates close for the night." Aaron threw his own hood over his head. It didn't hang as low as Brent's, but it did make his icy blue eyes even brighter. "We'll split into the same groups as before. Kro." He looked at him, stern. Then he acknowledged his inebriation and chose simple words. "Stick with your partner."

"I can go solo this time!" Kro argued with a barrel.

"C'mon, big guy." Kyrah grabbed him by the wrist and led him around the corner, deeper into the backroads.

Brent and Aaron disappeared down the middle road.

Erikk, Rhea and Liam turned down the final path, narrower than the rest, which forced them to hustle along in single-file.

The streets of Cleopa were emptying now that the day was ending. All along the thoroughfares and throughout the closing bazaars, citizens with all manner of hair colors were heading home. Heads of green, orange, pink, dandelion-yellow, and even white, bobbed down the streets, with the occasional brunette or blonde, and what with how their locks matched their brows and lashes, there was no doubt that such hues were actually quite natural. Indeed they were commonplace in the central province of Lenora, for no one seemed to think twice when they crossed paths with someone whose hair looked like the result of a curious dye experiment. The fact that everyone was wearing similar imperial wear — togas, stolas, tunics, sandals, armlets and the like — only further aided in the perceived normality of the populace.

Across the sky gentle shades of blue, pink and magenta banded the heavens, creating deep shadows that curved around the columns that supported porticos and offices. A shallow mosaic pool was fixed in the main square, each corner flanked by an ivory column, and flecks of the sun's fading light glanced off of its rippling surface.

This light was only countered by the shadow that was cast by the gates of Lenora Estate, which were more or less a colonnade that walled off part of the square and led to a miles-long avenue that led to the actual manor further away. Imperial soldiers guarded the towering arch that led to this path, spears aloft and armor glistening; one of them actually yawned. All was quiet at their post.

But news of the quarry raid was spreading rather fast everywhere else. Here and there, Brent and his splintered group were able to catch snippets of gossip that discussed the recent attack on the Southern Mines:

"I heard it was in the southeastern quadrant," a woman was caught saying just outside of Cleopa's largest administrative structure, a building on a high podium with a deep portico and a triangular pediment above marble columns.

"Do they know who did it?" someone asked her.

"Probably the same savages what coordinated that attack on Thom's Bridge last week."

"I hope those savages burn," an old man by a closing food stand growled. "They'll ruin our economy like this!"

"I heard *Skylok* was there," another remarked as he and his friend unloaded a cart of supplies to restock their store.

"Ain't it wanted in Lyrik?" the friend asked. "It was *here?*"

"Blaze and the Silver Shadow were there, too!" a little boy exclaimed to his friends near the city fountain. What with his dialect and elite manner of dress, the drawl of Lenora was absent from him. "But, I guess the Silver Shadow part might not be true. I hear no one actually knows what it looks like."

"I wish I coulda seen 'em," one of his playmates groaned, his social status just as prominent. "But my dad says they're dangerous."

"You mean they're inter-provincial?" another woman gaped, fanning herself in front of the city bathhouse as she conversed with a throng of well-to-do women. "Great, first there's threat of civil war in Brusseir and now savages are runnin' amok. This place is going to the dogs…"

"It's only a matter of time before Vicereine Aquila hears," Aaron said to Brent as the two passed by another grouping of imperials who were commenting on the raid. "She'll lockdown the city in minutes."

"Then we'd better get out in seconds." Twisting away from the road with a flap of his cloak, Brent ducked beneath a beam that was leaning against a wall in an alleyway and vanished.

Aaron ducked in after him.

The two regrouped with the others only a few roads away from the western wall of the city. From there, they blended into the trickling crowds that were filtering in and out of the capital — people who ranged from traveling adventurers to outgoing merchants — and crossed onto the paved road that connected to the royal highway. An extensive path that wove across the entire continent, it was what allowed the easy passage of officials and soldiers from one important city to the next — and for Brent and his fellow raiders, it offered a quick way home.

"There." Kyrah pointed at something farther ahead, right on the highway.

There, against the backdrop of the mountainous Peaks of Dover that ringed the barren plain just outside of Cleopa, a pair of imperial tradesmen were in the middle of an argument. A wheel on one of their wagons was broken and its driver was furious; the other, a thinner, slightly older male with baggy green eyes and longish brown hair, was desperately trying to calm him down.

"Why donchu look where you're goin'?!" the man with the broken wheel raged, his Lenoran accent thick in his fury.

"I really am sorry, sir," the other said, his hands up as if in surrender. His common, Arkanian intonation proclaimed that he wasn't of Lenora. "I was just trying to avoid that pothole…you know how the Empire can lag on their road repairs sometimes."

"What pothole?!"

"Is there an issue here?" A soldier came up to them, heavily armored with a galea helmet and a bulking breastplate. Gladius at his side he was intimidating, and had likely been called over by a concerned onlooker.

"Everything's fine, sir —" began the smaller man.

"Speak for yourself!" fumed the other. "D'you know how much fixin' these wheels is gonna cost me?!"

"Less than what you paid for them, I'm sure."

"You tryna start somethin'?!"

The soldier almost rolled his eyes.

As the two continued to quarrel, Kyrah guided her party around a massive gathering of boulders that was just beyond the highway. Coming around to the other side, where they were out of sight of anyone curious enough to watch the standoff, she and the others climbed into the cart of the man whose wheels remained intact. Being the last one to enter, Erikk drew the flaps shut.

Even as they had gone about with this stealthy operation the imperials had come to some sort of agreement, which resulted in the thinner man handing a sum of arkans to the other. Then, bidding farewell to both him and the soldier, he climbed into the front of his wagon, cracked the reins against the saigas that were hitched to it, and pulled off.

"Trent, you're either really clever or really unlucky," Aaron remarked from the wagon bed and with a shout, the man nearly leaped out of his seat.

Peeking over his shoulder, he twisted to get a better look at who was in the vehicle with him. His wide eyes sagged with relief.

"Oh…oh, it's you. All of you," he corrected, turning to face forward again. "And it's both: I thought to create some kind of ruckus to give you all a bit more time to get here. But while I was considering what to do, I nearly crashed into that man and, well, I'm sure you saw the rest."

"You shoulda broke his other wheel!" Kro said, then hiccuped.

Trent tossed a frown in his direction. "What's wrong with him?"

"What's not wrong?" Aaron cut.

Kro turned on him. "Hey —!"

Suddenly they hit a bump in the highway, causing the entire wagon bed to jolt.

Kro's cheeks bulged as bile surged up his throat. He keeled over abruptly.

"Keep it in!" Aaron shouted as the others voiced their own complaints.

"Quiet down!" Trent barked. "Bengai's not that far, you guys can't get along until then?!"

"He's the one about to vomit all over your wagon!" Rhea exclaimed, leaning away from the groaning Kro.

Trent rolled his eyes and faced the road with an almost dead expression. "And these are the best that Chief Ivan could send over…a bunch of kids."

"I'm twenty," Kyrah corrected, hearing him.

"My point exactly."

Brent, his hood now removed thanks to their being safely hidden in their supporter's wagon, smiled faintly as the bickering and bantering continued. Resting his back against the cart's covering, he tilted his head to peer out of the vehicle and into the world that existed beyond their driver.

Something soon caught his eye on the edge of a cliff to their right: a lone, black-clad figure was standing on the precipice, with a head of sleek, black hair that billowed in the evening wind. Their face was covered — by what he couldn't tell — but it seemed like they were looking in the wagon's direction.

He frowned, blinked.

The figure was gone.

His scowl deepened as they rode past the cliff. Then, leaning around Erikk, he hunkered over to the back of the wagon and brushed one of the flaps aside, allowing him to peek out at the mountainous terrain with one golden eye.

As they rattled past the cliff that had caught his attention, he scanned its peak.

There wasn't anyone there.

"Liam," he called, earning the Avat's attention.

Judging by the slow speed at which he opened his eyes, Liam had been in the early stages of falling asleep.

"Did you hear anything strange just now?" Brent asked, his eyes glued to the cliff as if the person he'd seen would re-materialize.

"No," Liam replied, his calm voice a stark contrast to the animated conversation that everyone else was engaged in. "Why?"

"Thought I saw something." Brent let the flap close.

"Maybe you need to rest. Lenoran heat can get to anyone." Liam closed his eyes again, and just like that began to drift off to sleep.

"Yeah…" Brent bumped the back of his head against the wagon's inner covers once again, his arms hanging over his lifted knees. "Right."

He stared at the upper frame of the wagon for a moment, contemplating. Then, succumbing to the fatigue that was at last conquering his adrenaline, he closed his eyes.

37

ROUND MIDNIGHT, BRENT was ripped out of his sleep by an eerie sensation that crawled all over his skin.

He shot up, grabbed his staff that had been lying beside him, and glanced about in the night.

He and the others had erected a small camp not long after darkness had overtaken the land. Cleopa was some miles to their backs, but with the fortified city of Bengai still miles away they'd opted to rest for the remainder of the night. It seemed a logical decision: after all the barren lands of Lenora grew treacherous as one ventured deeper into the wastes, threatening midnight travelers with hungry Trevian lions and wandering crocuta. Both were deadly — especially the latter, which were larger and far more fearsome than the first — and what with the group still worn from the raid, they'd prove to be easy prey.

Even Kro was in desperate need of a break, despite how much he tried to deny it. At present, he was snoring.

They were off the highway now, situated in the open fields right between the Peaks of Dover and the last of the looming mountains that made up the Southern Mines. The campfire was dying, only spitting out glowing embers every few seconds, and the rest of the group was still asleep.

That is, except for Liam.

At first Brent assumed that that was simply because it was Liam's shift for watch duty, which it was. But he quickly realized that something was wrong.

With his back to Brent, Liam was standing a short ways outside of the camp, sword drawn and feet spread. Thanks to the faltering fire his shadow flickered as it reached into the dark fields, and at its other end there was a quiet, murky silhouette.

Brent's eyes narrowed, adjusting to the gloom as he tried to determine what exactly the figure was.

It was a man, he could figure out that much at least, one whose body-configuring clothes were as pitch as black and accentuated his lean form. A waterfall of onyx hair dangled towards the small of his back but as for his face, Brent couldn't discern it.

Keeping a tight grip on his staff, he moved to stand next to Liam.

Liam's hood was off, and by the glow that fell from the full moon one could catch the soft luminescence of his bright eyes. The tension that he felt within was palpable in the air, an aura that was a far cry from his normal, almost vaguely indifferent demeanor, and strands of his hair tickled his furrowed brow.

"Maybe you weren't seeing things after all," he said quietly, his eyes never leaving the figure.

Brent said nothing, equally transfixed by the stranger.

"I didn't even hear him get close, let alone see him."

That elicited a response: an alarmed glance from Brent. What with there being no place for any potential attacker to hide in such an open field, it was a wonder that even Liam had missed them. The fact that he hadn't even heard the man's arrival was only that much more concerning.

Liam didn't meet his eyes. "He hasn't moved, though." He paused, waiting to see if his words would suddenly inspire the stranger to move.

He didn't flinch.

"He's just been standing there, watching us," Liam continued, keeping his voice at that same, quiet murmur that he thoughtlessly assumed the stranger couldn't hear.

Brent's voice was just as low. "How long?"

"Not even a minute."

"Think he's alone?"

"Very much so," the black figure said suddenly.

Both Liam and Brent flinched. Their arms locked, biceps flexed; Liam's blade flashed as he shifted, and Brent's staff howled when he flipped it into a ready position.

"Oh, don't worry." The man spread his gloved hands. His voice suggested that he was young, though still older than the auction raiders, and his tone carried a certain nonchalance, as if he was having a casual discussion with friends over a noonday meal. "I'm not here to fight."

"Who are you?" Brent demanded, his voice deep in his chest.

"Ooh, scary." The figure advanced, each step slow and deliberate.

Brent and Liam didn't shift their stances, but they did brace themselves for the worst.

"No…" The man stopped. "I won't fight you."

He was in better view now, and all at once Brent saw that he was wearing a mask. It only covered half of his face, revealing his brown chin and mouth, and by the contour of its features he concluded that it was meant to resemble a snarling, black lion. The spillage of black hair that fell from its crown was actually a thick braid that reached the wearer's tailbone, and dots of gray were painted just above its abysmal, black eye sockets. Other subtle markings lined its sharp cheekbones.

"A fight wouldn't get us anywhere," the man concluded, almost absently. It was a strange transition, as if something in the immediate area had caused his thoughts to wander for a second.

"Yeah?" Brent scoffed. No longer startled by the man's cryptic behavior, he dove into the reservoirs of his own confidence. "How 'bout we go a few rounds, then you can talk."

The man actually chuckled at the boyish challenge. It wasn't a cruel laugh, nor even a condescending one. He was genuinely entertained. "You may look the same," he started as his laughter quieted, "but you certainly don't act the same. Still" — another smile crossed his lips — "Çaru'qu doesn't make mistakes."

Brent's challenging stare made room for a hint of recognition and confusion.

"You're right, I'm babbling." The masked man waved a hand, shooing away his last statement. "I guess when I saw you of all people coming out of Cleopa, I had to come and see the sort of company you keep. Quite a diverse party of friends, I'd say. That much you do have in common."

Brent's wonder mounted, shown by the deepening of his frown. "What?"

"Are you with the Empire?" Liam stepped in. Though bearing a voice that wasn't as challenging as Brent's, its weight wasn't one to overlook. It was smooth but forceful, like a mist that rolled out of a waterfall to overtake a wood.

"Please! You wound me." The man grabbed his heart like he'd been struck there. "As if I'd work for the Empire. No…I'm just curious." He smiled mysteriously. "The last time Çaru'qu howled for someone in answer to global chaos, it caused quite the stir. I just wanted to get a good look at the one he's trying to summon to help stop it this time around."

Brent felt more than saw the man's eyes roll over him.

"You really are the spitting image of his last chosen," the stranger continued. "A fitting choice." His smile widened. "Couldn't have picked it better myself. Though, like the last guy…that probably means you've gone through hell to get to where you are now, haven't you?"

Liam's grim features were unchanged.

Brent regarded the stranger with an air of guarded suspicion. "What're you talking about?"

The man smiled wider. This time, his teeth shone in the moonlight. "I know all about what you guys have been doing across Lyrik. Across the whole Empire in fact: freeing the slaves and all that. Your people have been causing quite a commotion here in Lenora, too. And yet…" He brought a finger to his lips. "It's like you don't see the bigger picture at all. You're like children, only able to see what's right in front of you…and nothing else. To you, the Empire's only sin is racial tyranny. But maybe if you looked harder, you'd see something far worse." He seemed to be amused. "Don't tell me that you haven't yet heard it: the sound that warns of a coming storm. Çaru'qu's howl."

Liam maintained his guard. His stony expression was unreadable.

But beside him Brent faltered, for a certain memory had suddenly pricked his brain.

The night that he'd finally graduated into the ranks of the slave auction raiders of Taranis, he'd visited Adelle's grave. There, he'd had the strangest of daydreams: the world had been suffused in gold and green mist, the sky was open, a man with trailing, sky-blue hair had stood before him and a bodiless growl had barreled through the earth —

And then, just as suddenly as he'd seen it, the vision had ceased.

It'd happened almost a year ago now, and nothing like it had ever happened to him again. He'd told Aaron about it, and he'd also thought it was odd before he'd dismissed it as Brent having eaten something weird at the Feast.

Something had told Brent that that wasn't the case. Nevertheless, he'd dismissed it.

But now…

"I see you have." The stranger read the expression on his face. "So, I would continue to keep those sharp ears of yours open." Grinning wickedly, he pointed at Brent. "No telling when Ça-ru'qu'll think it's time to move. Ohh," he dropped his hand, "but you seem confused! Funny. I know I'm talkin' to the right guy, though."

Conquering his reservations, Brent clicked his tongue. "Quit talkin' in riddles and tell us what you want."

"I told you, I'm just curious!" The man shrugged. "But if you want a more definitive answer, maybe you should ask that chief of yours. Or better yet…the Elder's daughter."

That stirred something in Brent. He'd heard Xëri and members of the high council mention someone referred to as the 'Elder' before. As for who they were, he'd only been told that they were connected to the founding of the Liberation Fronts.

Their daughter was in Taranis?

"But I know she likes her secrets." The man tapped his chin. "So maybe the chief would be a better bet. What was his name again…" He smiled. "Ivan, right?"

Brent tensed.

"I've heard enough." Liam took a step forward and dropped into a battle stance. "Sounds like you know too much about the Liberation Fronts to just be 'curious'."

Brent joined him. "No kidding. Come quietly," he said, flourishing his staff, "or we'll take you down, no questions asked."

Surprisingly, the stranger laughed.

Liam's face remained hard.

Brent was just as resolute.

"Take *me* down?" The ghost of his laughter remained upon the man's lips and he bowed as if he was introducing a show. "Trust me…you wouldn't want to fight me."

Even as he spoke, a bodiless yet familiar pressure rushed over the raiders and a steady wind began to gather.

In a flash a windstorm was howling against them, its force so mighty that they could do little more than shield their faces. The grass bent, and a cluster of the green blades whipped into the air around the stranger, where they whirled like a tornado.

That same strange smile from before stretched across the man's lips. "Lucky for you, Çaru'qu seems to have plans for you yet. So I won't kill you. Looks like I'll have to spare your friends, too."

With one arm still lifted to cover his face, Brent squinted to see him. For a second, he thought he glimpsed one of his eyes —

It was teal and released a bright glow that pierced the gloom.

Brent's own eyes grew in bewilderment.

"Don't forget to talk to your beloved leader." The man smirked.

Another wind blew, harder than the others, and Brent guarded himself again. The winds raged for a second longer until, slowly, they began to die.

When it was finally safe to lower his arm, the man was gone.

Tight-lipped, Brent scowled at where he'd once been.

He didn't reappear.

"An aetheriest." Liam stood upright. "Should've known."

Brent didn't say anything. Rather, he dropped his eyes in troubled consideration.

"You didn't know him." Liam faced him.

"No," Brent said, loosing himself from his thoughts.

"But he seemed to know you. And I don't mean from wanted posters." Liam cast his eyes over the fields again. Though, with his vision being limited, especially at night, he was likely taking a second to listen to their surroundings. He could hear no hints of any other nighttime stalkers. "Better yet, it sounds like he knows about all of us."

He clenched his jaw. Then, he looked at Brent.

He seemed distracted, and Liam at once knew that he was deliberating over what they'd both just been told.

There wasn't any time for that though. "Well?" he asked.

Brent looked at him.

"It's your call," Liam said and he put his sword away. "Don't know if that guy's got friends out here. But we're sitting ducks either way."

"Right." Brent looked at the flattened field where the man had once stood. "…Let's get out of here," he said finally. "Wake the others."

With a wordless nod, Liam headed back to the camp.

Before turning to join him Brent looked out over the fields once more, beyond the winding highway and into the desert wastelands that undulated over the distant horizon. Then he looked towards the mountains, those shadowy giants that seemed to bear down on him with far more intensity than before. He strained his ears to listen to all of it.

He could catch the quiet chirping of crickets. Other than that, he could hear nothing.

Then again, based on how their recent visitor had arrived with not even Liam hearing him, it didn't seem like his Avat senses could offer them any better advantage.

And that was exactly why they had to keep moving.

Turning his back on it all, he joined Liam in waking everyone and assisted in repacking their belongings.

The sooner they got back to Taranis, the better.

Far above, on the edge of a cliff that overlooked their small campsite, the same man that had visited them perched along the edge of the precipice and watched them depart.

He smiled.^{tv}

KEEP TO THE CODE
CODE: CRISIS

38

THE REST OF the way to Lyrik Province, Lenora's westerly neighbor, was relatively uneventful. The Peaks of Dover tapered off into rolling foothills and then flat plains as they neared the provincial border. By the time Bengai appeared on the horizon, the sun had already climbed a few inches into the sky.

They only came across a few civilians on the highway, but when they found themselves about to pass slave traders or soldiers on patrol, the warriors in Trent's wagon grew quiet.

It wasn't fear that drove them to silence, but vigilance. After all they were still in Lenoran territory and with a bounty already on three members of their party — Brent, Aaron and Liam to be precise — they perceived that laying low, at least for the moment, was the best course of action.

Brent and Liam did tell the others about what had happened the previous night, citing it as the reason for their breaking camp hours before sunrise.

Aaron and Erikk were moderately surprised that neither of them had caught even the smallest breath of the interaction. But when Liam shared that not even he had been able to pick up on the stranger's arrival, they were troubled. The fact that neither he nor Brent knew where the man had gone afterward was only that much more disturbing, and the stranger's claim that he wasn't allied with the Empire did little to quell their concerns.

Kyrah, Rhea and Kro had no answer when Brent asked if any of them knew anything about aetheriests who wore masks that resembled black lions. Trent had no knowledge to offer, either.

"Saruke," he echoed, his Arkanian tongue shortening the word so that its foreignness would make sense to him. "For some reason that sounds familiar, but I can't really place it. Strange times we're living in, though: war is stirring in Brusseir Province, the emperor's demanding more sacrifices, and now vanishing aetheriests. Maybe that guy should join the Aether Circus."

"Guess all we can do is bring it up at the debrief when we get back," Erikk said. "But, hopefully it's nothing."

Brent shared the sentiment. But a pit in his stomach told him that it wasn't "nothing", especially when he considered the cryptic intel that spoke of a certain howling being a sign of him being chosen to ward off a global crisis. He could barely wrap his head around it himself and for that reason, he didn't mention that part to the others.

Liam seemed to have caught the unvoiced hint, for he'd kept that piece of intel to himself as well.

"Wait, what war?" Rhea asked, unable to move past Trent's off-handed comment.

"What, you mean Chief Ivan, the Brusseirian Bear himself, hasn't mentioned anything to you about what's going on in Brusseir?" Trent glanced over his shoulder and then shook his head. In front of him, Bengai's looming turrets and banners grew larger the closer they came to it. "The Katruskik tribes are acting up again. You have to have heard about their routine uprisings, at least."

"Well, yeah, who hasn't?" Rhea lifted an eyebrow. "The people in Brusseir lead uprisings against the Empire almost all the time, but they're always snuffed out since they're so small."

"And the people who lead them are always executed," Kyrah added gravely. "But after a couple of years, someone else takes up their cause and the cycle repeats."

"You can't really blame them," Trent shrugged. "Freedom is something that all people strive for, even if they don't want to say it out loud.

"Matter of fact, if you searched every town on this continent, you'd be hard-pressed not to find pockets of Arkanians who secretly hate the Empire, with its slave traders acting like they own everything, and then the heavy mandates for human sacrifices, which just creates a greater demand for slaves since people are forced to go through them so fast. Makes you wonder why the emperor wants so many of them sacrificed at all."

"Maybe he's just sick," Kyrah said coldly.

"Probably. And the Katruskik rebels would agree with you. They've been trying to boot the Empire out of what used to be the Kingdom of Katruska for centuries, but within the last few months they've finally decided to be more organized about it. To that end, they've formed a coalition between their tribes and are calling it 'The Katruskik Alliance'."

"Took 'em long enough." Aaron folded his hands behind his head and leaned against the wall of the wagon bed. "Can't say I was expecting an alliance though. Especially not between their tribes."

"Well, you know what they say: 'enemy of my enemy' and all that." Trent fixed himself on the driver's bench, feeling a bit stiff. "Word on the street is they've been giving Empyrean's Guard a hard time of it. Naturally, the Guard's decided to increase its presence up there, and of course that isn't making things any better. Hear the place looks like a military zone already."

"The Empire's always been good at making examples out of people," Kro put in. He'd had a terrible headache upon waking and still had an icepack pressed to his head, courtesy of Rhea and her freezing his waterskin. "If the guardsmen occupy all the towns in Brusseir where the Alliance is the most active, it'd discourage others from trying to join them. But" — he frowned —"if you're willing to call it a 'war', that makes it sound like they've actually got the skills to go toe-to-toe with the Empire this time."

"If you corner someone long enough, they'll show you their fangs." Trent rocked leisurely in the driver's chair, and his saigas snorted as they hustled along the cobbled highway. "With the way the Empire is, burning and looting peoples' property if they so much as sneer at the gods and our slave-based economy, well…you tell me how long a system like that can last."

"Four hundred years, give or take," Aaron offered dryly.

Trent's lips twisted into a bleak smile that none of them could see. "Not all that long," he mused, "when you think about it."

They didn't stop in the fortress city of Bengai when they came to it. As they neared its towering, aged walls and banners, they elected to cut across a side road and travel around it. There were enough supplies to last them the rest of their trip, Trent assured them, and there would be no benefit to their entering such a fortified city so soon after having caused an uproar only one town over. Given its fortifications, such as the gated archways and heavy military presence, if word of their entry got out the city would be locked down much faster than they could ever leave.

So they circled around its southern walls and pulled back onto the highway, which they followed back into Lyrik. The dusty terrain of Lenora swiftly gave way to the lush green of the Lyrikan fields as they went, and the craggy mountains morphed into grassy hilltops and tree-speckled valleys.

With their stomping grounds in sight the raiders began to relax, and as the second day of their travel came to a close they branched off of the highway and onto a dirt road that wound further west, deeper into the province.

By the time the moon had peaked and the stars were glittering on their third night of travel, they found themselves on a road that connected the coastal city of Peluma to a quieter town known as Ribbosheth. There, with no other soul in sight, Brent and the others bid farewell to Trent and leaped out of the wagon bed while it was yet moving. Swifter than cats they disappeared into the first wall of trees that made up Odelwhite Forest, a vast wood that bordered the fields just off the road. Deep in the web of interlocking boughs and shrubbery they made camp again, and by first light they set off to complete the last leg of their journey.

Deeper into the forestry they went, their way lit by mottled sunlight that broke through the canopy, and overhead the mountains that ringed the land they called home began to creep higher into the sky the closer they got to them. Over babbling streams they hopped and under gnarled roots they crouched, winding their way into the heart of the warm jade world.

At times they were forced to pause and blend into the greenery whenever an imperial was heard coming along, for the woods were a scenic hike for those in the nearby towns. But as they came closer to the belly of the forest, the number of these encounters dwindled until there were none whatsoever.

Finally, they came to a wall of entwined branches, flowered vines and closely spaced trees, all of which created such a tangled mess that it was impossible to see if anything was on the other side of it. Shrubs and lifted tree roots spanned the floor of its length, and the foliage was so tightly pressed together that not even the smallest of creatures could fit through. Its height was no less impressive, the wispy ends of its twiggiest branches coiling into the sky like wiry fingers.

Aaron passed his hand over this wall, his gloved palm causing the leaves to jostle. There was a quiet resolve in his gaze, a strong desire to move forward in spite of the obstacle that now hindered him. But he was no fool to think he could phase through objects, let alone squeeze through a barrier that was so tight.

Though, there had once been a time when he would've crawled beneath it, his narrow stomach pressed flat against the grass as he shimmied through a crawlspace beneath the branches.

Stepping back, he examined the lowest parts of the barrier and searched for the tiny hole that he remembered. It wasn't easy to find, for it was partway hidden behind a lifted root and curved beneath a hump in the land. He was almost certain that if he hadn't known what to look for, he would've never spotted it.

Perhaps a vulpi could've gotten through, he surmised, if it were a pup. He almost found it incredible to know that he'd once been small enough to squeeze through himself.

But those days were gone now.

Dropping his arm he turned to Liam and Erikk, who were standing a few feet away with their eyes fixed on the forest.

"I don't hear anyone coming," Erikk said at last. His shoulders loosened as he faced the others. "Hopefully that includes masked weirdos."

Liam looked at Aaron and shook his head, showing that he couldn't hear anything, either.

"Okay." Aaron backed away from the leafy barrier, giving Kro and Rhea some room as they came closer. "Guess you'll just have to be quick."

"You can't rush art," Kro said, spreading his feet. Lifting his hands, he held his left ahead of the right.

"Sure you can handle this, Kro?" Rhea asked warily, copying his stance.

"I'll be fine," he brushed her concerns, however minimal they were, aside. "Just try and keep up!"

"You guys sure you don't need a third?" Kyrah asked from their backs.

"Yep!" A cocky smile spread over Kro's face. "You can just take a breather, Ky. We got this!"

"Okay…"

Rhea exhaled gently. "All right…here we go."

She and Kro inhaled together and exhaled as one, and the hair on their skin rose as they turned their sights inward, each hunting for the quintessence that coursed within. Grasping it, they unleashed it, charging the air with an intangible force that sighed against their allies and caused the leaves to tremble.

Although he'd witnessed what the two were about to do countless times before, Brent still found himself enthralled by the quintessent disturbance. He glanced about curiously, as if he could actually locate the aether that Rhea and Kro were trying to connect to. Even though he'd seen it coming, he still felt a pang of disappointment when he couldn't spot anything supernatural.

An invisible force, the aether was what held the fabric of their entire world together. Everyone had the ability to connect to it, since every living thing held within it a spring of energy known as quintessence, which was believed to be the building blocks of the aether. By tapping into this pool of energy, one could connect themselves to the aether and perform all manner of impossible acts, from lifting objects that even the strongest couldn't budge to creating terrible storms, or conjuring fire out of nothing.

Those who'd been trained to exercise such abilities were commonly known as aetheriests. But not everyone could tackle such a role, for the training that was required in order for one to become an aetheriest was grueling and demanding. Due to the dedication required, there were only ten of them in Taranis.

So far as Brent knew, they all were proficient in different areas. For instance, Kyrah was particularly savvy when it came to levitation and invisibility, while Rhea was well-versed in almost anything that had to do with manipulating the earth. Heldar, designated their coordinator, was a force to be reckoned with whenever it came to blasts of fire and blinding light.

Even Kro and his brother Tyre had their talents, with Kro bearing limited talent in almost every area while Tyre excelled at creating whirlwinds with a flourish of his arm. In some cases, he didn't even need to move at all. On top of that, he could conjure barriers so powerful that not even a battering ram could break them.

Most aetheriests only specialized in one area or two, according to what Brent had been taught in Taranis' schoolhouse. But that didn't mean they couldn't at least learn other skills, as all of Taranis' aetheriests had already done. Supposedly, however, an aetheriest's limitations had something to do with the amount of quintessence that they were born with along with the kind of training that they were given. Both affected just how much they'd be able to do when they were linked to the aether.

Brent had tried to link to the aether himself once, long ago, before he'd ever even heard of Taranis. But he'd failed: rather than move a target, as had been his instructions, pure aetherial energy had exploded in his face.

A sign of rejection.

A sign of Avat blood.

After all, Avats and half-Avats alike were incapable of forging a connection with the aether.

Brent had only ever heard ideas as to why that was so, all of which made the issue "complicated", as Aaron had once said to him in the days of their childhood: Avats didn't have enough quintessence to spare when it came to linking with the aether; they'd been cursed centuries ago by an ill-meaning warlock; it was the punishment of Empyrean… The legends and allegories that went along with such answers tended to be convoluted, but creative to say the least. So to this day, Brent could only ever speculate as to why the workings of the world had deemed Avats unworthy of weilding such power.

If things were different, he was sure that the Avat people would've freed themselves from the oppressive hand of the Empire centuries ago. So many lives would've been spared and none of them would've ever had to suffer the abuses that they currently did.

But, that wasn't the world he lived in.

Nonetheless, he couldn't bring himself to hate the aether. He could only ever admire it and swallow the envy that struck him whenever he witnessed an aetheriest showcase their ability.

Like now.

But one thought did scratch his mind, even unsettle him: Liam had referred to the masked stranger as an aetheriest as well, and given how the man had both appeared and vanished, it was a sound determination. But when Brent compared the quintessence that he'd released to that which Kro and Rhea had released, he couldn't help but notice that there was a disturbing gap between their strength.

He found himself hoping that there weren't other people like that masked man in the world. If there were, and if it turned out that they actually were a threat to Taranis, he wasn't sure if even their aetheriests would be able to stand up to them.

"Okay…" The air settling, Kro stretched his hands towards the barrier of leaves and branches, as did Rhea. For a second, nothing happened.

At length, the moan of wood pierced the air.

Rooting himself to the present, Brent watched as the fortress that blocked their path began to curl aside, with every branch, vine and tree trunk bending as if they were made of elastic. Leaves rustled and bark groaned, and the roots that were twisting out of the earth creakily retracted. Gradually, the vast plains that existed beyond the wall became apparent, their rolling fields stretching beyond the shifting barrier.

"Almost there," Erikk said as the wall arched away completely, leaving the way into the mysterious valley clear. Passing a quick smile at the others, he proceeded to jog through.

Kyrah went after him and Brent, Aaron and Liam followed.

Kro and Rhea went through last. Once on the other side of

their forged gateway they refaced Odelwhite and pulled their hands towards their chests, drawing their quintessence away from the trees, out of the aether, and back into their bodies.

As their energy left it the wall returned to its former state: the trees curled back into place, their branches tangled, and the roots and shrubs shuddered back into position. When their reversion was done, not even a glimpse of the neighboring forest could be seen anymore.

Rhea dropped her shoulders with a sigh, her eyes closing.

"Heh." Kro brushed his nails across the shoulder of his tabard. "Nailed it."

The rest of their group was already venturing deeper into the valley, each of them hiking up the slight hill that would carry them to higher ground. Kro and Rhea joined them.

At its crest, all of them paused. For it was from there that they were able to see all of the landscape that carried a special place in their hearts.

There was green everywhere, existing in almost every known shade and pulling everything into a harmonious picture of nature at its best. Clusters of wildflowers claimed parts of the fields, adding pops of color to the emerald tones, and wild doranis wandered through them. Even from a distance the bucks were large and proud, with powerful bush-antlers that scraped the clouds. Not far from them does grazed with their foals, some of whom pranced after butterflies or wobbled on their knobby legs, and when one stumbled over a rabbit the creature's long ears irritably flipped into view.

Pine trees speckled the northern fields, walling off the road that led to the valley lake, and towering mountains ringed the sweeping hills. Forests blanketed some while others were capped with snow, and at the other end of the field stood yet another barrier of trees.

But these trees didn't mark the end of the valley. Rather they followed its center, splitting the vale in half and putting the village of Taranis in full view of the raiders.

It was a picturesque sight, with wooden houses crowning the hill that ran alongside the forested wall. Sunlight shimmered along the main road's stream, and villagers were nothing more than colorful dots that paced back and forth, visiting friends or starting errands. Some guided livestock to till the farmlands, and others groomed horses or fed domesticated saiga. In another area, it looked like the hunters were honing their archery skills.

It was so very different from the everyday Arkanian settlement, in aura more so than in appearance: there was no creeping sense of dread, not by the village nor anywhere else in the valley, and there wasn't even the slightest hint of imperial presence. There were no flags, no banners, no flashes of silver armor or billowing capes. There were no grimacing turrets or magnificent stone temples rising above the treetops, beckoning all to venture inside and bow to a bronze statue of the imperial god Empyrean, or even to the serpentine Vedrah.

It was better than all of that.

Brent smiled, a warmth growing in his chest.

Yes…it was better than the backroads of the city, the slummy streets, the threat of death and sleepless nights.

It was peaceful.

It was safe.

It was —

"Home sweet home," Erikk sighed.

"Yeah," Brent agreed.

That was it.

It was home.

39

"AND I TOLD you that it *isn't* a toy!"

"Yeah, yeah, whatever you say."

"Give it back, Boyd!"

"Make me!"

Lilian filled her cheeks with air and glared at the boy who stood a head over her. She lifted her shoulders and clenched her fists too, wholly mimicking the pose that she'd often seen Eklaire take whenever Aaron or someone else made her upset.

Boyd, a small boy in Taranis who was only a year older than she was, sniggered and tossed the beaded bracelet from one hand to another.

An Arkanian child, he was dressed just like the other members of the village, with a long sash that fell over his loose, blue-dyed pants like an asymmetrical apron, and a sleeveless top decorated with sewn-in mountains and hilltops. His brown hair shifted listlessly in a light breeze, and at his back his friends — or flunkies as Lilian preferred to call them — snickered.

The bracelet, a small set of circular beads whose uniform red was interrupted by a single jade stone, blinked in the sunlight as he tossed it.

He'd snatched it right off of Lilian's wrist while she'd been walking, startling her. At seven years old, most children her age would've cowered while the altercation commenced, fearful of standing up to the bigger boy and his bigger friends.

Lilian, however, refused to kowtow. Her uncle was one of the toughest raiders in the village. She wasn't about to let someone run her over.

"I said *give it!*" she shouted and she pushed Boyd as hard as she could.

With a grunt he hit the ground hard, and his bare feet actually flipped into the air.

His friends gasped.

"Ow…" Sitting up, he rubbed his back.

"It's not a 'stupid toy'." Lilian glared at him, fighting back tears. "It was my mom's!"

"Oh, your *mommy* gave it to you?" Boyd challenged, standing. He stood over Lilian again with a space-toothed grin. A tiny sliver of an adult tooth was growing in to fill the hole.

Lilian stood her ground. She could feel herself shaking, but she didn't falter.

Boyd made to speak again, only to pause when a shadow crept across the path and enveloped the both of them. He looked up.

Immediately his jaw dropped and his eyes grew.

Sniffling, Lilian turned around.

Liam was standing behind her, his eyes bright beneath the shadow that was cast by his hood. Not even his nystagmus, a condition of his albinism that was far more noticeable when his gaze was fixed, could eradicate the icy chill of his stare.

He looked from Lilian, to Boyd, to the bracelet that Boyd was holding.

He looked the boy in the face. "Give it back," he said.

Bug-eyed, Boyd shoved the bracelet into Lilian's hands. Then, yelling, he and his friends took off.

As Lilian fidgeted with her recovered accessory, Liam knelt to see her at eye-level.

"They keep bothering me," she said glumly. Facing him, she clutched the bracelet close to her chest. Her eyes were downcast, and her brown hair curtained her tan face. "He keeps making fun of me…"

"And you keep standing up to him," Liam said. He brushed away a tear that had collected beneath her eye. "He'll stop when he sees how strong you are."

Lilian sniffed and rolled the bracelet onto her tiny wrist. Squeezing her eyes shut, she threw her arms around Liam's neck and held on tight.

"I don't like it when you leave me, Uncle Liam," she said into his shoulder.

"I know." Carrying her, he stood up. "But I promised I would always come back, didn't I?"

"Mhm…"

"Hey."

Lilian leaned away to look at him.

He smiled lightly and tickled her stomach. "Guess who's back?"

Giggling, she hugged him all over again.

"Hey, they're back!" another villager called out, recognizing Liam and the small troop of raiders who'd reentered the village.

"They're here! They're back!" a child called to his friends, spotting them next. "Brent's back!"

"Brent's back?!"

"Brent!"

"I see him!"

"Rhea!"

"Kyrah, you're home!"

"Brent! Brent!"

The villagers, who'd once been focused on little else besides their daily business, suddenly set their growing excitement onto Brent and the other raiders. Erikk was quickly greeted by his elder sister, who clasped him into a tight embrace, and Kyrah and Rhea were pulled into a circle of friends.

"Good to see you didn't die, bro!" Tyre raised his arm at half-mast and clapped hands with his brother.

"Likewise," Kro returned. "Which is a surprise, considering I'm always the one who has to watch *your* back."

"They are back? Where are they?" The booming, raspy voice erupted from higher up in the village, causing some to glance around in search of the source.

Brent and Aaron did the same, with Brent looking from the boys and girls who were elated to see him while Aaron turned from a handful of younger scouts.

Chief Ivan was making his way downhill now, and his bearded face lit up when he spotted the raiders down below. Loosing one loud, solid laugh, he spread his arms and closed the space that existed between them.

Strands of gray were beginning to streak through his braided beard and hair, and the wrinkles that etched his forehead had deepened ever so slightly in the year since Brent had begun auction raiding. But he hadn't at all lost the delight of his character, nor the strength that rumbled in the base of his voice.

When Brent compared him to the man that he'd been when he'd first arrived in Taranis, the chief hadn't changed. He was still boisterous, still inspirational, still kind. They were qualities that Brent had grown to admire about him over the years, especially since he'd invited Brent into his home not long after he'd come to the village. After all the boy had been abandoned by whom he'd believed to be his only friend at the time, and there was no one else for him to shelter with.

Aaron was Ivan's only son and had been the one to find Brent initially, during an auction raid in the coastal city of Peluma. Brent was sure that had it not been for Aaron's intervention, Chief Ivan and his Avat wife, Xëri, might not have ever adopted him.

But he had, and now the rest was history.

A loving home and a dedicated family…given what Brent had suffered through prior to Taranis and the auction raiders, he hadn't ever believed that he'd be blessed with either. He never wanted to take it for granted.

Coming near, Chief Ivan greeted the returned warriors with handshakes that were more like arm-shakes, and hefty claps on the shoulder. With Rhea and Kyrah he was more gentle, but by the time he reached Brent and Aaron he cast off all restraint.

Laughing, he scooped them into his arms and squeezed. "Ah!" he exclaimed. "My sons!"

Brent thought his bones would snap.

Aaron gasped.

Ivan dropped them back onto their feet.

The two staggered, but more or less kept their balance.

"Is good to see you both!" Ivan dropped a hand onto their shoulders.

"You too, Dad." Aaron sounded a bit breathless.

"Yeah. Same here, Pops." Brent rubbed his chest.

Around them, some of the little children who'd witnessed the reunion laughed and giggled.

With a quiet chuckle, Ivan gathered a couple of them into his arms.

"Everything here all right while we were out?" Brent asked at the same time.

"Yes. All is fine." Ivan smiled at a little girl that he'd placed on his shoulder. She smiled back. "And all went well on the raid, yes?"

"Yep. And everyone who came with us is still accounted for." Brent thumbed his nose.

"Ahh!" Ivan's blue eyes sparkled. "Is what I expect! After all, Taranis has now best forces out of all Liberation Fronts, since you, Aaron and Liam have begun to work together. I expected as much."

Brent grinned proudly.

Ivan's words were true. In the months that had followed Brent and Liam's graduation into Taranis' forces only one year ago, the raiders' performance had improved dramatically. It hadn't been very long before the Liberation Front of Taranis began to lead the charge in the freeing of countless slaves across the western reaches of Lyrik Province, all but upending the Empire's ruthless enslavement of the Avat people in that region. It was a complete change of direction compared to their previous inefficiency, which had often resulted in the village losing as many warriors as slaves that they freed.

Truthfully, many if not all of their successes had happened under Brent's direction. Every mission briefing he attended saw him slip into the role of head strategist, and every raid that submitted to his tactical advice ended favorably. It wasn't long before his constant success had earned him a spot as one of the village's top strategists. The promotion had seemed to come quick but it had been hard-fought — most of Brent's ideas had been unconventional, to say the least. But in time, the veteran raiders had accepted that his fresh perspective was what they needed.

Along with this upgrade, Aaron and Liam had been made

permanent parts of his assembled squadron. Given his in-depth reconnaissance and highly-detailed memory of different locales, Aaron had become his official recon scout. Liam had been assigned as his official intelligence agent, due to his unmatched hearing as a Northern Avat.

With his friends' reports Brent's plans were often enhanced, enabling him to outmaneuver slave traders at every opportunity. More than once he'd led the shaming of decoy slave wagons, and with peerless diligence he kept track of when and where new but particularly strong slave traders were bound to appear in an effort to fend he and his teams off. He'd even switched up their operations by raiding stores that sold slaves like items in a knickknack shop, which upset the imperial economy even more.

Soon, the effect of his leadership began to manifest as a gradual dip in the number of raiders who were lost on missions. In time, it became such a rare occurrence that fear of it became rather foreign.

So, in the months that had followed, Taranis had experienced a population boom. With the number of raiders and newcomers no longer bearing a sacrificial relationship, the amount of villagers steadily began to rise. It wasn't long before the northern apartments couldn't house anymore rescues, and as a solution Chief Ivan had ordered for a new one to be constructed. Twice as large, it was a U-shaped structure that stood right next to the older complex.

To showcase their gratitude, and as every newcomer always did shortly after their entry into Taranis, the new villagers had volunteered for a wide variety of tasks in order to promote the village's prosperity. Some joined Taranis' raiding forces, drawing from their battle history as slaves in the Empire's coliseums, while many more became hunters or builders. Still others, claiming that they'd been educated by their masters, took to teaching at the schoolhouse, which was growing in its populace just as much as the village was in general. Eventually it, too, had been expanded. Carpentry, pottery, blacksmithing and weaving were other trades that saw increase.

Farming also grew in prominence, leading backyard gardens to be replaced with tilled fields that extended the village into the valley. Rescued slaves who were familiar with the agricultural process took to growing crops and medicinal herbs, as well as domesticating animals that were herded out of the neighboring woods and parts of the valley.

The original auction raiders and scouts were relieved by all of this, for it had lessened the burden that they'd been bearing for the past several years. With Taranis having once been a very tiny community, they'd had to perform multiple tasks in order to keep the village in order. But now, thanks to the growth and generosity of their new company, they could guiltlessly focus on their main tasks.

The only extra job they had to worry about now — at least, for the men — was hunting, which still needed a good amount of people to participate in order to feed the ever-growing community. Brent, Aaron and Liam weren't exempt from this responsibility, and so they'd often joined different hunting parties between their assignments.

There was also a spike in more unconventional trades, such as storytelling. Some of the rescued slaves were well along in years, and from them the children eagerly listened to tales that dated to ages long-past: stories of romance, mystery and myths; of the ways of the Avats before the Arkanian Empire; there were even anecdotes that the elders themselves had been a part of.

They also taught the children the age-old languages of their tribes, and although they were confused by the strange sounds that made up the words, the children — Avat and Arkanian alike — were astounded by them. Aaron had once mentioned that these elderly Avats were speaking different strains of Aionbo, an Avat tongue that he had learned from his mother and that Brent had consequently picked up while living in the chief's home. At times the two were able to interpret the words that the seniors were sharing, while at others they were just as baffled as the children who listened along.

So had Taranis prospered, and so it was predicted to continue to do so.

But things hadn't been positive all the time.

Empyrean's Guard — a faction of the imperial army whose sole purpose was to crush rebellions throughout the Empire — was weeding out the Liberation Fronts one by one. In every sanctuary village they upended, the people were rounded up and sold back into captivity, and the raiders who'd set them free were brutally tortured or sold themselves. In time, the number of Liberation Fronts had gradually been whittled down to six, as opposed to the original twenty that the group had started with decades ago.

Fear had crept its way into the ranks of Taranis' raiders as that point, causing many to question whether or not they should continue their rebellion. Many more were against such doubt and believed that, with the barriers that shielded their valley from sight — both natural and aetherial — they had no reason to be afraid. Chief Ivan and Brent had added their agreement to this argument.

So, Taranis had continued with their resistance until it had swelled to the size that it was now.

Brent had predominately been seen as the face of this change. In fact, by his eighteenth birthday in the early spring, which had only been a few months ago now, he'd become the most popular person in the village. Even children showered him with their adoration, and would drag him into games or impromptu sparring sessions whenever he seemed available.

It hadn't taken very long for the Empire to regard him as a considerable threat. What with his bright blue hair and golden eyes, his face became prominent on wanted posters throughout the imperial province of Lyrik — though, Brent and his fellow warriors saw it as more of a compliment than a concern. Even Ivan had been proud of him.

"Skylok" had been the title that he'd eventually been crowned with, an apt but straightforward name that Brent had grown fond of. Since he'd been raiding for at least a year more than Brent, Aaron had already gained his own title: "Blaze". His red hair and lightning-fast reflexes in battle had earned him the nickname, comparing him to a dangerous wildfire that engulfed everything around it. Given how he always managed to overwhelm multiple opponents at once, the title was fitting.

Liam had eventually gained the nickname "Silver Shadow", which truthfully had little to do with his eyes, for apparently no one in the Empire knew what he looked like. All officials were aware of was that there was some sort of suspicious character who seemed to disclose private information to the 'savages' that dogged the slave system. Whether or not this person was actually an outsider himself or some sort of double-agent hidden amongst their ranks, they weren't yet sure. But they seemed to believe the former.

Brent was proud of all of it, and even more grateful to be a part of any of it. He'd seen firsthand what the Empire was capable of doing to those that were born into the lesser ranks of society. That he could be an agent of change and offer hope to those people at all was more than he could have ever asked for —

And more than his eleven-year-old self would have ever believed to be possible.

"Don't fill his head with too much air, Dad," Aaron said in response to his father's reaction after hearing Brent's short report. He straightened his tunic. "Chief Anania couldn't stop praising him back in Dukaris. Any more and he might not fit through the doors at the Main House."

"At least there's the threat of me being too big for the doors, Shortstuff," Brent quipped, smiling impishly.

He knew he'd struck a nerve. Aaron had always harbored some bottled up resentment at the fact that although Liam and Brent had grown to be at least six feet tall, or just over it in Liam's case, he'd stopped a couple of inches short of it.

"Least I'm not a moonlicker," Aaron cut back.

"You'd rather stay a bootlicker?"

Ivan laughed, much to Aaron's annoyance.

"Bootlicker Aaron!" one of the children crowed.

"Bootlicker Aaron!" another one echoed.

"Say that again and I'll show you who licks boots!" Aaron said, stepping forward, and save those whom Ivan carried the children squealed and ran off.

"Brent! Aaron! Liam!"

Hearing their names, the raiders who'd been called turned to see a young Avat girl running to them. Her dark eyes wide with excitement, she hurried down the hill.

Another girl was coming with her, an Arkanian with short, wavy white hair and mismatched eyes of blue and green. Her lips, glossed with plant butters, were stretched into an elated grin as she came down the hill and the tassels of her ankle-length dress tickled her beaded ankles. She waved.

It was Harver and Eklaire.

Taking on work alongside her mother as one of the village seamstresses, Eklaire had become known around Taranis for creatively sewing an assortment of garments for the villagers, both new and old. She was a fast but tireless worker, and was known for creating more clothes than any thought possible within a week. She'd also come to dabble in jewelry-making, and each of her friends actually wore at least one accessory that she'd made.

Harver was equally diligent in her work as one of Taranis' most reliable engineers, and was often called upon to upgrade and design a number of gadgets for the raiders' missions. Given the increase in both raids and raiders, she and her colleagues were working overtime. But as taxing as it was, she still managed to work on her own, private project.

To be precise, it was one that she'd been in the process of fine-tuning since the summer of Brent and Liam's graduation. As for its name and what it would do she wouldn't say, but she boldly claimed that it would be so revolutionary, it would forever change the way that raiders and scouts approached their missions.

"Hey," Brent said when the two were close.

"Auntie 'Klaire!" Lilian exclaimed, and Liam set her on her feet.

Almost instantly, the child sprinted into Eklaire's arms.

"Hey, lil' darlin'!" She squeezed her tightly.

Lilian giggled.

"You're back!" Harver exclaimed. She hardly gave her friends a chance to return the greeting. "How was it? How'd it go? What was Dukaris like? Did the smoke blasters that I gave you work better or the same as the old ones?!"

"Did ya'll see the Peaks of Dover?" Eklaire tossed in, her blue and green eyes shining. Her Lenoran accent was a dramatic contrast to the Arkanian dialects surrounding them. "I've been goin' on'n on about what ya'll might see with Harver'n Ren since ya'll took off. I ain't been to Lenora since I was knee-high to a grasshopper, and even then I only got faded memories bouncin' around in here." She rapped her head with her knuckles and her eagerness seemed to mount. "Well? Don't just keep us waitin', how'd it go?!"

"Uh...it was good," Brent started and he looked from Aaron to Liam as if he expected one of them to elaborate on the details for him.

"Dukaris was dark," Liam said plainly.

"The new smoke blasters are better than the old ones," Aaron added.

"And yes, we saw the Peaks." Brent smiled at Eklaire.

Harver and Eklaire stared at them expectantly.

The boys didn't add anything else.

"What, that's it?!" Eklaire finally blurted.

"You guys suck at recaps," Harver said disappointedly.

"We answered your questions!" Brent protested. "What, you want a play-by-play?"

"That'll have to be saved for the debrief," Aaron pointed out.

Harver threw her head back and groaned.

"Fine," Eklaire pouted. Her round, childlike face made her scowl impossible to be intimidating.

"Yes, the debrief must be had. And sooner than later." Ivan set the children he'd been holding down on their feet, much to their disappointment. "We will go to conference hall in Main House," he said decidedly, nodding shortly to Kyrah, Erikk and the rest of Brent's team as they crowded around the leader. "I will hear your report there."*tv*

SAFE RETURN
CODE: HOMEATLAST

40

THE CONFERENCE ROOM that Chief Ivan had spoken of was on the second level of the Main House. Windowless, it was large enough to host at least fifteen people, with tawny lanterns screwed to the walls and a long, oval table placed in the center.

Up against the back wall, a small banner hung from the ceiling to the floor. A symbol was emblazoned upon it, made up entirely of interlocking and disconnected rings that gleamed in the firelight.

The logo had become familiar to Brent after he'd first arrived in Taranis, and he'd since learned that it represented the Liberation Fronts' mission: the hope of uniting the slaves and all of those who were oppressed by the Empire into realms of safety, contrasted against the opposing reality of their forced disunity. It was also woven into the villagers' clothing; even he and his friends had it woven into the patterns of their own outfits.

As per custom Chief Ivan took his place at the head of the table, right in front of the banner, and laid his large hands upon it. The young raiders dispersed, with Brent and Aaron taking a position at either of his sides while the others took up posts next to them.

At Ivan's indication, Aaron initiated the beginnings of their report. He started with the ease with which they'd been able to link up with Trent, then moved into their arrival at The Waterhorse, the Lenoran inn that was run by another supporter and whose labyrinthine cellar connected them to Dukaris. He then segued into their first interaction with Chief Anania and her warriors. They'd been skeptical of Chief Ivan offering them such a young team but, having heard of Brent, Liam and Aaron's reputations far ahead of the encounter, Chief Anania had calmed her people into hearing Brent's strategy. Eventually they'd fallen into agreement, and Brent's plan had been executed successfully.

"Chief Anania did have her doubts, though," Aaron added. "Just like she said in her scout's letter, she wasn't sure about asking for help because she was thinking to relocate the people of Dukaris entirely, since the Southern Mines were digging close to their tunnels. Their forces aren't as strong as ours, so if there'd been an encounter she was sure it wouldn't have gone well.

"We checked it out, and sure enough the imperials were getting close to the village. If we'd gotten there maybe a day or two later, they would've found it and called in the Guard a second later. Luckily, that's not how it ended." Though his eyes glinted with pride, Aaron didn't allow the emotion to overtake his somber expression. As the chief's son, he'd learned that there was a time and place for boasting, and a debriefing session in the Main House's conference room wasn't it. "Kyrah, Kro and Rhea collapsed all of the mining tunnels during the rescue. It's unlikely that the Empire will try to reopen them, least not anytime soon."

Ivan grunted his understanding. "So, Liberation Front of Dukaris is safe, for now."

"For now," Aaron confirmed. "And hopefully for a long time."

Ivan's smile showed through his beard.

Aaron concluded with their return to Trent and their journey back to Lyrik. The authorities weren't alerted to any of them being in Cleopa, he stressed, though there was a chance that they'd been cutting it close.

"But for now, Vicereine Aquila doesn't know that three of Lyrik's most wanted were right under her nose," he said. "All credit for the attack will go to Dukaris, but she won't be finding them for a while yet."

"In and out, just like we promised," Kro put in.

"Mm." Ivan nodded. "Good. And you are all accounted for. There were no casualties, or serious wounds?"

"None that couldn't be handled with a few bandages," Rhea answered.

"Good."

Brent turned from Liam, with whom he'd just shared a short but intentional look, and faced Ivan. "There's one more thing."

Ivan looked at him expectantly.

"After we'd left Cleopa, we decided to camp not far from the western Peaks," he started. "I'd say about midnight, we were…visited by someone."

Ivan's bushy eyebrows almost met.

"I was keeping watch at the time," Liam picked up, earning the chief's undivided attention. "There wasn't anybody else nearby, but then out of nowhere someone was standing just outside the camp, watching us."

Ivan immediately pinpointed the strangest part of Liam's account. "You did not hear him approaching?"

Liam shook his head soundlessly. "I did feel something, though. I think it was the aether. Brent woke up not long after that."

"The man who showed up was wearing a mask," Brent added. "A half-one that looked like a Trevian lion. He…" Brent frowned at the table. "He talked like he knew me. He didn't say much, just that…'Çaru'qu doesn't make mistakes.' Don't know what he meant." He glanced around at the others. "None of us do. Neither did Trent. The name sounded familiar to him, but he couldn't place it."

Ivan stood straighter, the motion slow and careful. With his bright blue eyes fixed on the table, he seemed to be analyzing Brent's story in one part of his brain while the rest of him sifted through thoughts and memories that he could run parallel to it.

"After that, he vanished," Brent continued, watching the chief attentively. "And not like, slowly-disappeared-as-if-he'd-made-himself-invisible. I mean, he hit us with this blast of quintessence that was like a tornado. When it was over, he was gone."

Ivan stroked his beard thoughtfully. "Did you see this man again?" he asked.

"No." Brent shook his head. "I had the team break camp. Every night after that, we set two people on every watch. One was always an aetheriest. But that guy didn't show up again."

Ivan was quiet for a moment, thinking, rubbing his beard.

"D'you think he might've followed us?" Erikk asked, looking around the room at everyone. "Should the night watch get beefed up?"

"This man," Ivan began, pocketing Erikk's concern, and his distant eyes returned to the room. "You say he spoke as if he knew you?"

Brent nodded seriously. "And I don't think he knows me as Skylok. But I couldn't recognize him from a hole in the wall. As a matter of fact," he continued, "he knew about all of us. The Liberation Fronts, I mean. What we do. Why. He even mentioned you by name."

Ivan's face darkened and his frown deepened until the folds in his brow looked like trenches digging into his skin. His large hand stopped moving across his beard and Brent noticed something glaze over his eyes. It was concern, but there was no fear connected to it. In fact, the chief looked more pensive than he did troubled.

Brent didn't remark on it, but he did bear this reaction in mind.

"You ever hear of it, Chief?" he asked, sticking to the leader's proper title given the context of the room. "This thing called Çaru'qu. Or even anything about who that guy was."

"An old acquaintance, maybe?" Rhea dared meekly.

Once more, Ivan escaped his silent musings. "Çaru'qu," he began, "is a legend. Old…myth, dating back to time before Empire. Imperials believe that, at one point in time, their gods walked among the people. They lived with them, and taught them things of the aether, and how to build societies. Çaru'qu, according to some stories, was one of these gods."

"But the Empire only worships two gods," Kyrah pointed out with a skeptic frown. "Empyrean and Vedrah. There's supposed to be another one?"

Ivan bobbed his head uncertainly. "Yes…and no. Empire does not recognize Çaru'qu as same as Empyrean or Vedrah. While some tales acknowledge Çaru'qu, he is said to have opposed the other two. Others even say that he was stronger than the both of them."

"Wonder why Arkania would ignore him, then," Kro said. "I've heard plenty of those old legends back when Tyre and I lived in the Empire. Even schoolkids knew 'em. But I've never heard of this 'Çaru'qu' guy in my life."

"Hear, hear," Kyrah agreed.

Ivan grunted. "Is no surprise. Stories of Çaru'qu go so far as to say that he once battled with Empyrean and Vedrah, millennia ago, in several violent wars, and that he emerged victorious every time. Does not look good for Empyrean and Vedrah."

"Odd…" Kyrah remarked quietly, touching her chin. "Arkania's an empire of conquest. Can't imagine why they'd want to go and worship two immortal losers."

"Guess if we wanted to know the answer to that we'd have to talk to their founder," Aaron said dismissively, folding his arms.

"You mean the dead guy?"

"My point exactly."

"Is strange that this man in mask would mention Çaru'qu to you, Brent. Out of…how you say…blue sky." Ivan looked at him, his grave expression hard under the low lighting. "Was there anything else that he said to you?"

Liam set his eyes upon the strategist, waiting.

Brent hesitated. "No," he forced out and he looked away. "That was it."

"Hmm…" He could feel the chief's suspicious look boring a hole through the side of his head. But, to his fortune, the great leader didn't press the matter.

"Erikk," he said, changing his focus, "your father is leader in night watch. Tell him that I request he increases village security."

"Sir." Erikk nodded.

"Rhea, Kro and Kyrah, remain here with me. And Aaron, summon Heldar." He paused. "And tell Yuan to summon head council."

"Sir." His son nodded stiffly.

"The rest of you are dismissed." Ivan laid his hands on the tabletop once more. "Thank you for your report."

"Hey…do you think that increasing village security will really help?" Erikk asked as he followed Brent, Aaron and Liam to the lower level of the Main House. While large and spacious the building was only two floors high, with the conference room and storage areas for maps, archived reports, and imperial disguises on the upper floor, while the lower hosted the kitchens and a vast dining hall. Evenly spaced bench tables lined the wide room, and sunshine filtered through the windows to lay squares of light upon the polished floorboards.

The delectable smell of broiling doranis and wild hen was already wafting through the air, likely to serve as a part of the Main House's daily buffet for the residents of the northern apartments, and several volunteers were busily cleaning in preparation.

A handful of the apartment dwellers had already arrived but were entertaining themselves while they awaited their meal, with some sitting down to chat over a light snack from their rooms while others engaged in gossip, or played tabletop games made of wood-blocks and stones.

"Aren't you the one who suggested it?" Aaron asked in pointed response to Erikk's uncertainty.

"I know, it's just, I gotta wonder," Erikk returned worriedly. The four of them gathered in the middle of the hall, and he looked between Brent and Liam. "I mean, if a guy like that aetheriest really showed up in Taranis, d'you think we could take him?"

"Let's just say I hope that day doesn't come," Liam replied.

"That's hardly comforting…"

"Sorry to disappoint you."

Erikk's troubled look spoke for him. "Guess I'm just not too familiar with any of this. I wasn't raiding for very long before the Liberation Front of Evanis was discovered by the Empire. It's a miracle me and my family made it out and found Taranis at all…"

"Then take it from us," Brent said, clapping a hand onto the young man's shoulder. "Try not to overthink things that're ahead. You can only prepare as much as you're able. Maybe we're outmatched, but if anything that guy's outnumbered."

"I guess…" Erikk stared at the floor, crestfallen.

Aaron sighed. "I don't like the thought of being attacked any more than you do, especially if we're talking about an aetheriest that can sneak up on us without even Liam hearing him. But it's a problem to deal with when it gets here, if it does. All we can do is prepare. Dad's gonna tell Heldar; maybe he'll beef up the aetheriests' training."

Erikk looked from one of them to another. A small laugh blew through his lips. "You guys are the real deal, all right. No wonder you're seen as the Big Three. It's like nothing can faze you."

Brent, Aaron and Liam exchanged looks.

"Big Three?" Brent repeated.

Aaron shrugged.

"Just a nickname I've been hearing the trainees use for you around here." Erikk shooed the matter away. "Anyway, guess I'd better go and find my dad, fill him in."

"And I've gotta look for Yuan and Heldar," Aaron added. "I'll catch you guys later."

"I'm gonna check on Greta," Liam said as Erikk and Aaron headed for the exit. "Lilian mentioned that she was sick while we were gone. She might need me to grab some medicine for her from Khirsta."

"Think you'll need help?" Brent offered.

"No."

"All right, then." He frowned when he realized that Liam was scowling at him. "What?"

"You didn't report on everything that happened that night," he pointed out bluntly. "Not to Aaron and the others, or to the chief. I played along. Now I wanna know why."

"Oh, that." Brent sighed, his eyes lowering. "Pops…he knows something about that masked guy, I can tell that much. But as for whatever that something is, it won't be easy to get him to talk. Still…what he told us about Çaru'qu is helpful enough. But it puts a heavier weight on what that guy said: global chaos, being 'chosen' to fight it…it's a lot to wrap your head around."

"What'll you do then?"

"I'll fill Aaron in, and we'll see if we can't pry a bit more intel outta Pops. But I'm gonna need you to keep an ear to the ground. Maybe some of the elders know more about this forgotten god than the rest of us. I'm guessing this is the first time you've heard about any of this stuff, too."

"Yeah. And with everything else that's been going on in the Empire…guess it'd be pretty dumb to ignore it."

Brent nodded his agreement.

"I'm gonna get going," Liam finished. "I'll tell you if I hear anything."

"Right. Counting on it."

Leaving him with a short dip of his head, Liam headed for the doors.

"Oh, I thought you'd heard! Renée works so hard, but Terra's gotten a lot more protective of her lately. Apparently, she wants the girl to stay at home rather than join the frontlines with her and Ben!"

Brent felt his ears tingle, and he couldn't help but look to where the voices were coming from: a small trio of women who were seated a few tables away from him.

"Oh, that's right," one of them recalled, sitting up as she remembered details related to the juicy topic. "Elliot, my son, is always raving about how she's one of Jeffrey's top students, and I always catch her working up a sweat during her private sessions with him. It'd be a shame if she couldn't graduate…"

"It would've been great if she'd been able to graduate alongside Brent and Liam last year," the third woman interjected. "Y'see how those two and the chief's son turned out after training with Jeffrey since childhood? Renée's gotta be just as great. If she'd been allowed to join Taranis' raiders with them, things would look even more amazing than they do now!"

"She is a tough girl, just like her mom," the first woman mused, dropping a cheek into her hand. "It really would be a shame if all that ability went to waste…think of all the slaves that would have to be left behind!"

"Have either of you seen her today?"

"Last I heard she was still at the sparring hall…"

"That girl, always working hard!"

One of them glanced over at the door when it swung open, and there was a flash of blue as someone stepped out.

When Brent pushed open the doors of the sparring hall, he stopped in surprise at what he found.

Two people were clashing swords in the middle of the earthen floor, which acted as the sparring hall's battle space. The squeal of their blades bounced between the wooden walls, ricocheting until the entire building was echoing with the sound of war.

Panels of wooden flooring were flushed against the walls all around the hall, and a group of trainees was seated on the righthand side. Most of them were a few years younger than Brent, while others were just a bit older. Those of the younger class were transfixed on the action in front of them, as if the fate of the world depended on its outcome. By comparison, their upperclassmen kept turning to each other to offer commentary.

Closing the doors and keeping to the shadows, Brent watched the match with interest.

One of the fighters, a girl with black hair twisted into a bun, danced out of range as her opponent rushed her with a violent flurry of attacks. When he tired at last, she pivoted on the ball of her foot, switched the hold on her sword and circled towards him. Her blade weighted with momentum, she snatched the upper hand of the fight, forcing him back this time.

The girl was Renée.

Brent lifted his eyebrows a bit.

Her golden skin glowing with sweat, Renée's split bangs were stuck to her face and the hairs of her feathered and beaded hairpiece clung to her shoulders. The tail of her waist sash and its accessories spiraled with her quick, circular movements, and puffs of dirt kept flying by her sandaled feet.

Her footwork was impeccable, her stances sublime, and with every attack of her opponent she protected herself with a rock-like guard. Given how her training partner towered over her and was bulging with physical strength, her ability to defend, attack and parry was praiseworthy. Her speed was his bane, and his strength was little more than a mirror that reflected the superiority of her own expertise. Truthfully if their fight had a moral, it was that size didn't matter — skill, however, did.

Brent smiled quietly, impressed.

Her growl rising in a crescendo, Renée locked her sword with that of her training partner. Burying her feet into the ground as she carried the weight of his last attack, she threw him over her head.

Brent's mouth, as well as that of the students, dropped.

With an explosion of dust and dirt, Renée's opponent fell face-flat on the earthen floor behind her.

The students winced.

So did Brent.

Swiping her sword across the air, Renée sheathed it at her side. She exhaled quietly.

Then turning around, she set her sights on her teacher and waited for his verdict.

"Good." Jeffrey, her main sparring instructor, nodded from the side of the room opposite where the students had gathered.

Dark-skinned, round-eared and bearing a strong build, he boasted a presence that was just as staggering as it had been when Renée had first met him as a little girl. A pair of Arkanian raiders that were close to his age were seated on either side of him, having taken up roles as supporting instructors in the last few years. "You leveraged your enemy's weight and force against him. The last time I saw someone your size hurl someone that big over their shoulders, it was your mother on a raid out in Bengai. She flung that soldier like he was a sack of wheat, armed with nothing but that stiletto and gauntlet of hers." His narrow eyes flitted to the trainee that Renée had just thrown.

He was delicately picking himself off the floor.

"Seems like the apple doesn't fall too far from the tree." When Jeffrey looked at Renée again there was the smallest hint of pride in his gaze, a rare occurrence for an instructor who'd proven to be a rather stoic character around his pupils. "You're making fine progress, Renée. The frontline forces of Taranis will be glad to have you."

Renée perked up a little, as if Jeffrey's dollop of praise was something she'd been earnestly longing for. "Thank you, sir!"

"That's enough for today. I'll see you for your private lesson tomorrow."

"Yes, sir."

"Ulrich."

"Yes, sir?" Renée's partner sniffed as he got up, still catching his breath.

Jeffrey studied him for a second. "Clean yourself up. You've got work to do on your stances. Meet me here again in twenty."

"Sir." Nodding to Renée, who nodded back, he moved to depart.

"The rest of you are dismissed," Jeffrey called to the other students, who began to chatter amongst themselves as they recapped Renée's battle.

It wasn't long before one of them got distracted by a shadow in the corner of her vision. Turning aside from her friends, she recognized who it was instantly.

"Brent's here!" she cried.

"Brent! You're back!" one of the other students burst, running to the villager, and the rest of them followed suit, barraging the warrior with questions and exclamations of his name in an effort to get his attention.

"When did you get back?!"

"Brent!"

"You're okay! I knew you'd make it back!"

"You gave those stupid slave traders another butt-kickin', huh?!"

Already drawn by the ruckus, Renée turned to see that Brent wasn't far from the doors of the sparring hall, smiling as the students hurriedly surrounded him. The youngest ones had made it to him first, with whom he shared high-fives and hellos, while the older ones he greeted with chin-up nods and forearm grasping.

Reaching up to fix her bun and better secure it, Renée approached him. Halfway there, one of the younger boys called out to her.

"Ren!" he shouted, and her eyes leaped over to him. "Ren, Brent's back!"

It was Mekial, her younger brother. Fourteen years old now he was still enlisted in Jeffrey's classes, but had been making excellent progress over the years. Their father, Ben, praised his growth and talent, and seemed delighted that both of his children were growing to be strong warriors who would bolster Taranis' growing forces. His hair was still short — or at least, shorter than most of the village men who opted for undercuts and bangs — and his big, brown eyes were glowing.

Grinning, the boy pointed at Brent excitedly.

Renée followed his finger and locked eyes with the blue-haired Avat.

"'Sup?" he said, smiling.

"Welcome home," she greeted, returning the pleasant expression. Her hair secure, she dropped her hands. "I'm glad you're safe."

He smiled handsomely, grateful for her words. Then, he puffed out his chest. "Nothin' to it!"

She gave him a hopeless smile, but he could tell that she was entertained. "You and Aaron are like two peas in a pod."

"Brent! Brent!" Mekial moved closer so that Brent could see him. "Did you see Ren's sparring match just now?"

"I did!"

"Wasn't it awesome?!"

"It was!"

"Yeah! My sis can kick butt!" He punched the air. "I wish you'd gotten back earlier. Then you coulda seen my match! Jeffrey says I'm a natural!"

"That so, huh? Pretty cool." His gaze slipped over to Renée again.

She smiled, one shoulder rising. "He's got a few good tricks."

"A few?" Mekial burst. "I won my fight! I've got tons of tricks!"

"Try not to share too many of 'em," Brent said, tousling his hair. "You've gotta keep some surprises for the imperials, right?"

Mekial grinned. "They'll never see me comin'!"

Brent smirked, and looked up sharply when he heard Jeffrey address him.

"Good to see you're back safe," the man said, coming nearer to the group. "But I hope you don't intend to clog up the only way in and out of the hall."

Brent grinned sheepishly, one hand rising to scratch the back of his head. "Right — when Jeffrey says class is over, everyone's gotta clear out. C'mon guys, grab a bite, take a bath. If you hurry, you'll get first dibs on what the Main House's staff is cooking up!"

"It's almost lunch!" Mekial exclaimed. "Mom said she'd save me some roasted doranis if I got home in time! C'mon, Ren, you don't wanna miss out!"

"Okay, okay," Renée laughed as he and the others began to file out of the room. "I'll meet you there."

With one last, broad smile that had grown to become a characteristic expression of his, the boy hurried out of the hall with his friends and classmates. Brent and Renée trailed at the end of the crowd, leaving Jeffrey and the other sparring instructors inside.

"Not much longer, now," Brent said, looking down at her as they went.

"Hm?" She looked up at him, her eyes round and questioning.

"The Feast of Liberty," he reminded her. "You'll be graduating with a few others, right? You've gotta be excited to finally be able to get out there."

"Oh…" The light in her eyes faded a little. Lacing her hands behind her hips, she passed her gaze to her feet.

Connecting the dots, Brent figured out the reason behind her discouragement. "Is it Terra?"

"She just…" Renée sighed and stopped walking.

Brent halted beside her, waiting.

"Ever since Empyrean's Guard was set up by the military, she's been against letting me or Mekial finish our training," she said, her eyes still cast aside. "And now that my graduation is coming up, she's been even more uptight. We fight a lot…" She hugged herself. "Me and her."

Brent raised an eyebrow.

Renée noticed and almost rolled her eyes. "Not with swords!"

Brent snickered. "Wouldn't put it past ya."

Renée punched his arm playfully. A brief second later, concern caused her brow to furrow yet again. She rubbed her arm. "Her and dad are the ones who inspired me to be a raider. To want to help people the way that they do. Still, she just…" She sighed again, her arms falling. "She still doesn't think I can do it."

Brent offered her an apologetic look.

"I know she's just being my mom." Renée started towards Taranis again and Brent fell into step beside her. "But it's starting to irritate me. I have to prove myself to her…somehow. And even if Empyrean's Guard showed up…" Her pace slowed as the weight of that possibility crawled through her veins, starting first in her feet before it ascended to her stomach. "Whether I was out in the field or not, I'd still be in trouble. Wanting to learn how to defend myself and those I care about shouldn't be a crime." She looked at him in earnest. "Don't you think so?"

It was a simple inquiry, but it pried into the recesses of Brent's mind all the same, weeding its way through the memories that he'd long-since buried and tucked away from those around him: of being mistreated and objectified, of being cast aside like unwanted merchandise and the near-total theft of his humanity…

He'd often wished it had all gone differently. In time, he'd reasoned that if he'd been able to fight, or if he'd taken more initiative in protecting himself and the one that he'd cared for the most at that time, it probably would have.

Maybe.

His lips twitched with a smile that just barely hid a certain pain that felt both foreign and present at the same time. "Couldn't agree more."

Renée stared at him for a second, troubled. Breaking eye contact, she continued on to the village.

While she most certainly knew how to carry herself in battle, Brent couldn't help but notice the femininity of her stride. She walked with a certain sense of resolve that breathed through her shoulders, and an unmistakable confidence that swayed across her hips.

He felt his face get hot.

Turning aside, he fixed his golden eyes on the houses that moved to box them in as they neared the main road.

But the image of Renée's gait was already burned into his brain.

"I'm gonna clean up," she told him, stopping to face him once they'd arrived at the bustling hotspot that was the main road. Children were playing by the stream, villagers were chatting on doorsteps, and those who worked in the lower farms were carting vegetables to and fro. Off in the distance Brent could hear the muffled clanging of blacksmiths at the forge, and elsewhere they both could discern the hammering of someone repairing a leaky roof. "See you around?"

"Yeah." He nodded.

She smiled. "I really am glad you're back, Brent." Tossing a hand up in a short farewell, she turned and jogged away.

He only watched her for a second before he set his eyes on the rest of the village. The crowdedness of it all hardly bothered him, nor did the jumbled mix of conversation or the short instances of eye contact that he made with passing villagers. It was all refreshing, comforting after his tense interaction with the Empire over the course of the past week.

Closing his eyes he took a deep breath, taking in the smells along with everything else. When he opened them, his lips were already rising at the corners.

Lifting his head he stepped forward, adding himself to the activity that was thrumming in his midst.

It was good to be back.

41

THE AVAT WOMAN screamed into the torchlit chamber, a horrible cry that bore in it all of the agony that tore through her. Thrashing and shaking, she tried yanking herself away from it — but there was nothing she could do to free herself from the iron clasps that bound her wrists, nor from the chains that attached them to the grimy, stone wall behind her. Even her legs were bound, held to the floor by iron cuffs that held her on her knees.

She screamed again, her back arching, and her black hair spilled away from her eyes. Slowly, the pull of gravity in the room began to increase, causing the thick walls to tremble and the ground to shake. Pebbles danced across the stone floor.

The woman screamed once more.

Almost utterly bored, Emperor Koberius watched her.

Two imperial soldiers stood on either side of him, each armed with spears. Their helmets, glowing like molten gold, bore the head of Empyrean on their brows and a hissing Vedrah beneath it, and their breastplates imitated their muscles underneath.

Beside them there was a third figure: the same woman who was only ever seen at Koberius' side whenever she did appear. Dressed in a pale chiton with detached sleeves, her jet-black hair spilled over her shoulders to reach her waist. Armbands of silver hugged her upper arms, and her face was entirely guarded by the shadow of her separated hood.

One of the guards shifted uncomfortably when the Avat unleashed a blood-curdling shriek.

By comparison, the hooded woman was as stiff as rock.

Even Koberius was silent.

At last the Avat arced her back again, her elbows bending inward, and she clenched her teeth. Flashes of gold and tints of teal peeped through her squeezing eyes, and she clenched them shut. Small stones drifted into the air right after, upset by a strange imbalance in the atmosphere, and locks of her hair began to swirl upward with them.

Electricity darted through the air space.

Koberius' eyes narrowed.

The woman struggled again, every vein in her body protruding, throbbing. More electricity crackled around her, flickering like lightning.

Koberius' eyes began to widen. But then, just as quickly, his boredom returned, this time rimmed with annoyance.

The woman screamed horribly and the chamber shivered.

The weight that had once filled the room began to warp, forming pockets of pressure that distorted her cry. Light began to exude from her body, a tranquil turquoise glow at first, and then it began to brighten until it sought to bear resemblance to the sun.

Stiff-faced, Koberius crossed his arms over his chest and then spread them outwards.

Specks of light flickered in front of him before smashing together, solidifying into a barrier that curved around him, his bodyguards, and the hooded woman.

No sooner had his shield gone up did bolts of electricity, wind and light explode out of the Avat and crash through the chamber.

Koberius' hair and the tail of his sash billowed behind him. For a moment he and those with him were lost to the ensuing light, until it faded and kingship was given to darkness.

Koberius dropped his shield, which dissipated like stardust. Sweeping his arm across the smoky air, he forced the glittering specks to vanish altogether.[tv]

He snapped his fingers.

Fire crackled to life in the blown-out torches, filling the cham-

PATIENCE, A VIRTUE
CODE: EXPERIMENT

ber with their glow. By it, he studied the room.

It was still intact, although in some places shards of stone had fallen to the ground and black scorches existed where they hadn't been before.

If things had gone the way they were supposed to, the damage would've been worse.

He would've preferred that.

Even so…

His golden eyes revolved to the unmoving Avat. Wordlessly, he approached her.

One of the soldiers started. "Your Excellency!"

The second guard joined him. "Emperor Koberius, the body could still be dangerous —!"

"Shut up." Koberius' voice, though calm, struck his guards like knives. He stopped just a few paces short of the woman.

Her head was bowed into her chest and her arms were sagging at her sides. Trickles of blood were leaking out of her sharp ears.

In the quiet and the shadow where the torchlight could not touch, Koberius' mouth curved into a dark and sinister smile. His eyes, however, remained hard and dangerous.

"Your Excellency." The cold walls of the chamber seemed to resonate when the woman in black offered up her voice. "If I may: there is a chance that the goblin's body was simply unable to react to the drink. They are without quintessence after all; there was nothing for the aether to latch onto. It may as well have been an empty shell to begin with."

Koberius' amusement disappeared as the woman spoke, likening itself to a glare that he leveled with the dead Avat. Lifting a hand, he clawed his fingers and twisted his wrist.

The chains shattered, sending shards of metal flying across the floor.

The Avat promptly fell over. Her empty eyes, half-lidded and leaking tears of scarlet, gazed at the emperor's feet.

"I have no choice but to start from scratch." Koberius looked upon the dead woman, the torchlight casting harsh shadows across his face.

Tilting his head, he spoke to his guards next. "Take it away."

"Highness." Together, the guards approached the fallen Avat and took her by the arms. Then, they dragged her to the dark doorway on the other end of the chamber.

The hooded woman watched them go without so much as a word.

At her back, Koberius lifted his eyes from the ground. Then, slowly but surely, he began to laugh.

Silently, the woman faced him.

Koberius' chuckling mounted in volume, his shoulders shaking, and soon the room was filled with his laughter. He ended it with a quiet gasp of delight.

"Foedia," he turned to her, the ghost of his smile lingering on his lips. Paired with the callousness of his eyes he seemed cold, despite his obvious amusement. "You didn't see it, did you?"

The woman, Foedia, started to speak. But she stopped herself, realizing what he was referring to. By the firelight that barely touched her scaly skin, Koberius saw her eyes flash with surprise.

"Yes…" Koberius' smile became wolflike. In his own mind, he recalled the instant where the Avat's eyes had glittered teal and gold.

The eyes of an aetherian.

"Will you disperse this new draft through Empyrean's Guard then, Your Highness?" Foedia questioned. "Its effects could be beneficial."

His grin fading, Koberius regarded the woman with a distant, yet considering look. "Yes…" His eyes seemed to ice over. "That would move things further along, wouldn't it? But…" All at once, his countenance was disfigured by another devilish grin. "We'll need to ensure that that new 'Katruskik Alliance' can keep up, won't we?"

⤙ ⚶ ⤚

"'Çaru'qu doesn't make mistakes.'" Xëri echoed the phrase quietly as she gazed over the amari tree hilltop. But rather than face the east, where the mountains ringed the fields and led to the barrier that bridged their realm to Odelwhite, she faced the west. There, the valley extended towards the mountains that walled off the back of their hidden region, dividing it from the wilderness that waited beyond. In the open sky overhead, stars glittered like diamonds and the moon waned amongst them. "A proverb of the Order of Zion. That man said that to Brent?"

"Yes." Ivan, who was standing not far from her, approached to be at her side. He turned his bright eyes in the same direction as hers. "It has been a long time since I heard someone say it."

"The Shades don't normally reveal themselves so openly. But, it seems like ever since Brent arrived here they've been loosening their own restrictions. Almost as if he's..." She trailed off.

It was a while before she continued. "You know...I'd always kept Oruviçu's warning in the back of my mind. For all these years." A soft wind sifted through her wavy red hair and she brushed some of it behind her ear. "That Brent's arrival here may be dangerous to us somehow."

"I remember," Ivan nodded, recalling the evening that she'd informed him of shortly after it had occurred. It had happened almost seven years ago now. But given the nature of the conversation, not even Ivan could bring himself to disregard it.

"I know I made it clear that we had no intention of abandoning Brent," his wife continued. "And Oruviçu hasn't brought it up again. Though by now...I'm sure my father is aware of what we've done. But the fact that he hasn't done anything about it makes me wonder..."

She trailed off and Ivan looked at her to find that she was staring at the earth, lost in troubled thought.

"I am sure Elder has his reasons," he assured her. "But, yes..." His bright-eyed and encouraging look began to dim and he, too, became pensive. "Is all...troubling."

Xëri made a small sound of agreement. She didn't look up. "'The last time Çaru'qu howled, was in the days of the Aether Wars'," she recited softly. "'In the days of Zion. In the days that the gods roamed the earth.'" Her brow furrowed as she considered her budding theory. "What if...what if Çaru'qu is howling again now...for Brent?" She looked at Ivan, as if seeking confirmation on her idea. "Like with Zion? But the last time that happened...the

reason was because Empyrean and Vedrah…and the world were…”
Her confidence waned. Biting her lip, she stopped and looked away.

Quietly, Ivan took her hand. “Xëri. Do you remember when we first started Liberation Fronts?”

She gripped his fingers and a small smile tugged at her lips. She looked at him again. “Well, it was more your idea than it was mine.”

The light in Ivan's eyes didn't falter. “But you encouraged me to start. And helped me to build this village. The first of many. And we said…” He waited for her to finish.

She held his hands. “We said…that we would bring freedom to all the Avats,” Xëri recalled tenderly. “Even to those who weren't, but who wished for a world of unity and the chance to live their lives freely.”

“Yes. As Zion and your people said: ‘hope of unity, in midst of disunity’.”

Xëri nodded again and traced one of the patterns on his vest with her hand. Circular with intersecting and broken bands, it represented the very idea that he'd just recounted.

Ivan caught her chin and gently urged her to look at him. “This has not changed. The Liberation Fronts' mission is still the same. Though we have lost many brothers and sisters along the way… hope for freedom will never die.”

Xëri smiled and leaned her cheek into his hand. “You're right. I know. I just can't shake this feeling I have…” She pulled away from him with growing distress. “A feeling that says that maybe… there was more to what Oruviçu said. He mentioned a night that would've made us change our minds about Brent, but he's never explained it. It's like it haunts him. I wonder if it's connected to why a Shade would say that to Brent so suddenly…”

“Hm. Well…being honest,” Ivan began, “I cannot imagine scenario where I would think less of Brent. He is like Aaron to me. He is family. He is my son.”

Xëri nodded quietly, her lips drawing into a tight smile. “Yeah. He's our boy.”

She couldn't imagine thinking any different, either. Brent had been the second son that she and Ivan had always wanted but had never been able to conceive. He was a blessing that they hadn't expected. A gift that they'd never asked for, but would never surrender.

"And no matter what happens…no matter how" — Ivan gestured with a strange flailing of his arm towards the western mountains as he fought to find the right word — "Çaru'qu howls or how the world may change, nothing will change that. And nothing will change our mission. And so, we will continue, as we have. With Brent. As we do."

Xëri nodded again. It was obvious to Ivan that she was still uncertain about the things that she'd mentioned, but it was just as obvious that she wasn't about to let it overcome her.

"For as long as we are able," he said, pulling her into him, and together they looked out over the western plains, and towards the stars that glittered over the world beyond. "No matter the howling. Or what Oruviçu says. Or what Elder does."

"Right." Xëri leaned against him and sighed. She felt her body unwind a little. "Right…"

And she closed her eyes, breathing in the night air as she focused on the present: on Ivan's touch, on the gentle winds passing over the hilltop, on the sweet smell of grass and leaves, on the fact that there was no danger at that present moment.

For as long as we are able.

She hoped that that would be for a long while yet.

⚘

Working meticulously, Aaron shaved off a shred of wood from the tiny sculpture that he was carving. The piece landed atop his desk, where a pile of the paper-thin scraps had already gathered, and it was swiftly joined by another when he whittled the figurine down further.

Raising it so that his lantern could better illuminate what he was making, he turned it around in his hand.

Behind him, his bedroom door creaked open.

He didn't look up from his work. Lowering the little sculpture and leaning back in his chair, he kept on sculpting. "Don't you knock."

"Like you've got somethin' to hide," Brent quipped, entering.

"How 'bout some basic privacy?" Aaron carved his sculpture up a bit more. A few swipes here and a sizable chunk removed there, and it immediately looked like a feminine hand.

"What's that?"

"Eklaire wanted something to hang her custom bracelets off of." Aaron put the figurine down on the table he was at, above which there was a shelf of other small creations that he'd made over the years. From what Brent understood some were gifts, and others Aaron had made while he'd been bored. All in all, the hobby was a pastime for him when he wasn't preparing for a raid or training.

Setting his knife down, Aaron looked at him. "What is it?"

Brent shut the door. He looked serious. "I have to tell you something."

❧ ✲ ☙

Embers and smoke floated listlessly as the masked man crossed the wide study, their undulating forms sourced from the inferno that ran wild throughout the mansion. Against the roar of crackling flames and smoldering wood, his booted steps were calm, rhythmic; they would have been better suited for a peaceful stroll along a pier after dark.

At his back the bodies of soldiers and servants spanned the marble corridor, their blood seeping across the floor to reflect the destructive flames and singed banners, the smashed statues of the head of household and nude figures of myth. They'd barely put up a fight.

Or, perhaps the masked intruder had simply been too strong for them.

"P…please…please don't! I'm begging you!" Caught in the recesses of his burning study, Lord Elkiah of Orinn pushed backward on his smoldering, tasseled carpet. His wispy blonde hair and robes disheveled, he spread a hand — his only form of defense — as if that could ward off the stranger that prowled towards him. "P-p-please! I'll give you anything, anything you want! Arkans? S-s-slaves? What do you want?! Just say it!"

The man before him, dressed from head to toe in body-configured clothing and limited armor, said nothing. Framed by the fires that blazed in the hallway at his back he stared at his victim, peering at him through the dark holes of his mask.

It was a ferocious accessory, hiding its wearer's entire countenance, with a grin of knife-like teeth that rose towards its snarling cheeks. A wild mane of black hair erupted from its crown, falling towards the wearer's hips, and in the middle of its forehead there was a golden symbol, consisting of interlocking lines and curves that Elkiah didn't understand. In his hand, he carried a single curved broadsword that was unlike any weapon the imperial had ever laid eyes on, but it gleamed just as brightly as any other sword would in firelight.

An unrelenting fear seized Elkiah as the man came closer, ensnaring him before he could even think to escape it.

"Please!" he screamed, tears beading in his eyes. "I'll do anything!"

Still his intruder said nothing, only looked down at him with that grinning mask of his.

When he was only feet away from the imperial he lifted his sword, the angle of his grip shrieking what he meant to do with it.

"Please, no!" Elkiah begged. "Please! I beg of you, have mercy…!"

At that, the man froze.

Then, finally, he spoke. His low voice was even despite what he'd fought through to reach Elkiah, as if facing off against teams of trained soldiers had hardly even been able to make him sweat.

"I'm sure," he started, "that your slaves begged for mercy once, too. The ones you beat. The ones you had your way with."

Elkiah whimpered pitifully, tears beading in his baggy eyes.

"But you imperials aren't familiar with that term," the intruder continued darkly. "Mercy."

The nobleman squeaked.

The intruder didn't miss a beat. "I'm not either."

Elkiah's eyes swelled.

And the man's sword came down, gleaming like molten lava, arcing towards Elkiah's flesh the same way it had come down on his soldiers.

When it cut into him, it cut into the man's scream, too. In a flash, both were gone.

When the nobleman's body had fallen, slumped upon the bloody, carpeted floor, the stranger swiped his sword off to the side, flinging splatters of blood onto the desk.

One could only wonder if he was grinning as terribly as his mask.

The Avat Prince will continue in Volume 6...

WATCH <u>FREE TALES OF ARKANIA EPISODES</u> ON THE MVP TV YOUTUBE CHANNEL!

THE AVAT PRINCE: VOLUME 6

I'VE STUDIED YOUR records extensively, Murdoch," the emperor told him. He lifted his head to look down at the man and his golden eyes were caught by the sunset. "You've served the Empire of Arkania as a slave merchant for most of your adult life. You're dedicated. Loyal. Honest."

"Y-y-you flatter me, Your Majesty." Even though the emperor couldn't see it, Murdoch hastily wiped his foolish grin off of his own face.

Koberius didn't respond to the slave trader's remark. "Your report," he continued, "describes some similarities that seem to exist between the devil you saw seven years ago and Skylok. So imagine my surprise upon learning that one of the last slave traders to have interacted with Skylok is also the same man who drafted this uncanny report? I simply had to meet you and confirm it all for myself."

Murdoch could hear a chilling smile in the young man's voice. He swallowed yet again and for some reason felt a pang of disappointment. Even though he'd already known it, he was a little disheartened to learn that the emperor's summoning really had nothing to do with a promotion. "M-my lord."

"So, Murdoch, I must ask you this next because, being confined to the walls of the palace, I'm unable to determine certain things for myself. But from what I hear it's believed that this devil, this… Skylok, has blue hair. Much like the devil from your report. Is this true?"

"Y-yes, Your Highness. That's true. I saw it with my own eyes. I-i-in fact…and, perhaps it's my own memory playing tricks on me, but, I'm almost certain that Skylok is the same devil from my report, Your Highness. So far as I know, blue hair can't even be found in Lenora…I'm sure it was the same one."

Koberius' eyes narrowed threateningly and his lips thinned into a straight line. His hands were so tense that the bones were visible through his skin when he clutched his armrests. "It would seem, Murdoch…that you and I are the same, in a way."

"S-Sire?"

"Years ago I, too, encountered a devil with blue hair and golden eyes. I had just claimed the throne…and it was a child, whose father had dared to hide its existence from me." Koberius stood, and the motion was so graceful that the folds of his tunic and wrappings shifted around him like streams of silken water.

Murdoch swallowed so hard it was as if he'd eaten a rock.

Koberius lowered his chin to peer down at him. "So I have just one more question for you, Murdoch Macrinus of Northern Lenora."

"S-Sire." For a reason Murdoch couldn't quite place, he dared to lift his head once more.

His heart stopped.

From the shadows where the emperor stood a pair of gleaming, golden eyes were peering right back at him. It was as if he was being pinned by the horrible glare of an insatiable beast.

Murdoch gulped again, and now that he was looking at the throne he noticed that a strange figure was standing just behind the emperor's right shoulder, ghost-like thanks to the way the shadows clung to them from the waist down. A studious glance revealed that the silhouette was that of a woman, but as for her exact features they were just as obscured as the emperor's, bathed in the darkness that was cast by her wide hood.

But even with her face absent to his gaze, Murdoch could feel her stare boring into him as intensely as that of the emperor. It was as if she willed to cleave him in half with it.

And if he wasn't mistaken, her eyes were little more than two scarlet gems sitting in the hollows of her face.

One of the palace guards standing next to him forced his head down, and he saw no more.

"If you were to take your best guess," Koberius continued darkly, and Murdoch suddenly found it harder to breathe; the air in the room felt like it was being compressed from above, as if something was gradually sitting on top of it, "would you claim this devil of yours to look anything like Lyrik's provincial ruler, Viceroy Diomedes?"

CONTINUE READING IN
THE AVAT PRINCE: VOLUME 6!

About the Author(ess)

Myranda V. Peterson

A young artist who wears many hats, Myranda Victoria Peterson is an author, illustrator, animator and voice director with a contagious passion for storytelling. She first started off writing plays, which her parents and friends helped her perform when she was a little girl. A self-taught artist, her creative work is heavily inspired by anime and Japanese pop culture. She creates original, high-fantasy content that aims to inspire the youth of today with themes of generosity, courage, friendship and hope.

Myranda is the founder and CEO of the independent imprint and joint animation studio House MVP and lives in Boston, where many famous, classic authors have gone before her. She hopes that one day, her name will join them!